STONE VALLEY SERIES:

A Place in His Heart

The Wilderness Bride

The Lady of North Star

Sand Castles

The Crossing

STONE VALLEY SERIES:

Book #3

THE LADY OF NORTH STAR

By

DONNA WHITAKER

Model for front cover: Nicole Daley
Photograph of Author Donna Whitaker by: Glenna Drew
Photograph of cover by: Griffin Ball
Cover Design: Griffin Ball

∞∞∞∞∞∞∞∞∞∞∞∞∞∞∞∞

∞∞∞∞∞∞∞∞∞∞∞∞∞∞∞∞

All scripture quotations are taken from the
King James Version of the Bible.

Dedication:

To Glen.

CHAPTER ONE

KENTUCKY, 1794

AS SHE WAITED IMPATIENTLY IN HER FATHER'S CABIN, Rachel Templeton drummed her fingertips on the roughhewn table in the middle of the small room.

"Rachel!" exclaimed her father John Winslow, interrupting her thoughts. "Stop that racket!"

She immediately stilled her fingers.

"Sorry, Pa," she replied.

Rachel shifted a little in her chair and stared at him quizzically as he moved about the one-room cabin in aimless agitation. Something was definitely wrong. He was jumpy and tense and she'd never seen him this way before today.

"Do you know what Sam wants to see me about, Pa?" Rachel asked, still probing her father's features for some hint about the secrecy of this meeting.

John shrugged his massive shoulders as his eyes shifted uneasily toward the heavy door.

Her own eyes followed his and she thought some grim beast might break through it at any time.

A beast? Sam Spencer?

"Sam has been downright unfriendly to me at times," she thought, "but a beast?"

"It's none of my business," John Winslow finally replied, his eyes dropping to the empty mug in his hand. "That's between you and Sam."

Bending down to the hearth, John lifted the pot and busied himself refilling his wooden cup with hot coffee.

"But surely you must—" Rachel started a protest, and then silenced it as her father's look defied any further questions.

For a few moments Rachel sat slumped at the table, looking into the fire, confused. Why Attorney Sam Spencer wanted to meet her in her father's cabin was beyond her.

They had recently arrived at Stone Valley and her chores were endless. Quickly building a small cabin to accommodate herself, hired hand Frank Morgan, and his wife Louise, there was still land to clear to make ready for crops in the spring.

Sam Spencer's insistence on meeting at her father's place irritated her.

Of course, everything about Sam irritated her.

Oh, he had been polite enough, but never displayed any real warmth toward her.

In fact, Sam Spencer maintained an aloofness bordering on outright frigidness that bewildered Rachel at times. His slights had stung her on more than one occasion, forcing her to bite her tongue.

Meeting him back in Wellington, Virginia, before their journey, was pleasant enough, but something apparently happened afterward that caused him to turn frosty with her. She had racked her brain, trying to figure out what it was about her that he found so distasteful. To this day, she still didn't know.

Resigning herself to the fact that she would get no information from her father, Rachel looked about the room as if seeing it for the first time. Only one window—tiny at that—let in light. A small sideboard nestled beneath it, on which were two wooden plates, one mug and utensils, all whittled by him. A rope bedstead with a pine tick stood in a corner.

Unlike her own larger cabin, packed in every nook and cranny with items shipped down the Ohio…his was spare.

She drew a deep sigh as her eyes flitted over the skirt of her dress. It was torn from the brush she and Frank had cleared away, and she made a mental note to find the time to mend some of her frocks that were quickly becoming unsuitable to wear. If she didn't think Frank would disapprove, Rachel would have slipped on her britches for such hard work long before now.

Not that Frank ever said a word one way or the other. He was calm and easygoing, never criticized or complained, and often she caught a glimmer of admiration and approval in his eyes as they worked shoulder to shoulder.

But goodness! How often the inconvenience of her attire brought her to the brink of marching to the cabin and grabbing her trousers. She determined at such times to put aside her pride and stop wearing skirts…at least on the farm. But fear of what he would say always made her back down. So each time she ended up vowing to herself, "Someday, but not today."

The farm took all her time, and she had little time for anything else, certainly not for wearing pretty dresses.

Besides, she had nowhere to wear them. She had not been to the nearby recently established town of New Wellington since her first visit there, for, in general, she paid little heed to what was going on in the outside world.

"Pa," Rachel said, her finger drawing imaginary circles on the table, "Do you know if any kind of social is going on in town?"

"Oh, you know Mrs. Templeton and her committee ladies," he replied with a half-smile. "In spite of all the building going on, I'm sure they've found some reason to have one."

Rachel arched her back and she rubbed the back of her neck with her hand. She'd been working so hard and was so tired that she would welcome a respite from her responsibilities.

Frustrated, she blew out her breath and nearly jumped from the table, prepared to make her exit. Her arrival in Stone Valley, Kentucky only six weeks earlier had occasioned a frenzied effort to set things in order before the harsh months of winter arrived, and she had no time for Sam Spencer's frivolities.

Her five hundred acres, obtained from Colonel Wellington's land grant, adjoined the five hundred acres her father owned on the West side of her farm and the five hundred acres Sam owned on the East side.

Rachel was proud of what she had accomplished in such a short time. With the aid of Frank and his wife Louise, she had been able to quickly raise a log cabin, clear an area for next spring's garden, and cut and stack enough firewood for winter. But there were still fences that needed to be built for her herds, land to be cleared, fruit from the trees that needed preserving, and much more to do.

Rachel's brow furrowed into a frown.

Where is Sam, and why does he want to meet me at Pa's?

Rachel scraped back the chair, stood up, and walked to the small, unadorned window, noting that the trees were struggling to turn into the customary kaleidoscope of autumn colors. The unusually dry, hot weather of August and September had turned some to dull, lifeless colors and a number of trees had already lost their leaves.

It was an unusually warm October morning, quickly approaching afternoon, and she had no time to waste for whatever *business* Attorney Sam Spencer had with her. Dropping by her cabin yesterday, he had been vague when she asked why he wanted to meet with her...particularly at her father's cabin and not her own.

"An important business matter" was all he would offer. Peppering him with questions, Rachel grew suspicious when his face set in martial lines as he refused to give her any insight.

She had never had much patience, and this "business matter" had turned over and over in her mind until she slept very little during the night. Either it was something too complicated for her to understand, or he had, for some reason, been afraid to speak of it until today.

CHAPTER TWO

LATER THAT MORNING, THE SOUND OF A HORSE'S HOOVES pounded heavily on the hard earth, coming furiously as though someone was on an urgent errand.

Rachel jumped from her chair, wondering if some disaster at North Star had brought Frank with bad news. Crossing hastily to the window, she saw it was Sam, hatless, the wind catching the locks of his flame-red hair.

Drawing his horse up abruptly, Sam sat for a moment lost in thought before slowly dismounting. She watched as he unlatched his saddlebag and drew out several papers, glanced at them, and struck his hand against the saddle.

What on earth?

She listened for his footfalls and knock on the door.

At the sharp rap, John Winslow crossed the room and opened it.

"Come in—come in, Sam," he stammered nervously.

Rachel eyed Sam warily as he stepped inside, his wide shoulders filling the doorway, blotting out the sun's rays streaking through the branches of the nearly bare trees.

How tall he was—as tall as her father and as tall as Ransom had been! As always, her first glance into his arresting, cornflower-blue eyes gave her a little shock.

Unbidden, memories of Sam's behavior on the trail stiffened her spine, and Rachel folded her arms, kept silent, and looked at both men suspiciously.

Sam offered her a semblance of a smile and a curt nod. "Sorry I'm late," he apologized as John shut the door with a decisive thud. "I had a mare to foal this morning."

Declining the mug of coffee that John offered, Sam laid the papers on the table.

"The reason I asked you to meet me at your father's place, Mrs. Templeton, is the fact that he can confirm some financial situations that have to do with you."

Financial situations? And he's calling me Mrs. Templeton instead of Rachel?

An alarm sounded in Rachel's mind and her dark eyes sharpened suspiciously.

At something in Sam's eyes, she looked again at the papers on the table, growing uneasy. Cocking her head, Rachel looked up, her eyes curious, yet measured, and searched Sam's eyes again as though she would find an answer to this mysterious appointment.

She had traveled with him on the road here from Virginia, but she didn't really know him. She found herself on guard whenever she was around him, and she didn't like the feeling.

John moved to her chair and holding its back, said in a tone that she had learned to obey, "Rachel, I think you need to sit down. This is important."

Important, he says.

Her curiosity about this meeting finally trumping her dislike of Sam, she moved slowly to the chair and sat down. Sam seated himself in the only other chair and John leaned against the fireplace, noisily sipping his coffee.

Sam cleared his throat and spread the papers before him on the table.

"I'll get right to the point. What you see before you, Mrs. Templeton, is your husband Ransom's Last Will and Testament. He had a premonition that something was going to happen to him on this trip, so he asked me to draw this up for him before he passed away."

Her eyes darted to the document.

"Of course," he continued, studying her thoughtfully, all too aware of her wariness, "the five hundred acres you are occupying are yours since he specified this was to pass to you. But there is another matter he was concerned with."

Another matter?

Pausing, while a muscle worked in his jaw, he extended his finger to another provision on one of the papers.

Rachel's eyes fastened on Sam's pointed finger. Was his hand shaking ever so slightly?

She must be mistaken. Sam Spencer was never rattled.

"The matter of the proceeds from your farm in Virginia that was sold...Ransom stipulated that I am to be executor of the will and trustee over your estate and money until the time that you turn twenty-five years old."

It didn't register immediately and Rachel stared without as much as a blink.

Sam measured his words carefully as he continued. "In other words, Rach—Mrs. Templeton, I am to have absolute say over your financial affairs until you are twenty-five. You must come to me for any money that you need and according to Ransom's will, I am to have absolute power over your property and how your money is spent."

He looked up at her. "Do you understand?"

Her face drained of its color as the shock of what he had spoken tried to register in her mind. Slowly the light of understanding began to dawn in her eyes.

"My money? Sam has control over my money for what...eight more years? This can't be real. It just can't be. It's a nightmare. Surely, I'll wake up and find it's all a bad dream!"

At her stunned stillness, Sam hastily continued on. "Of course, I have my own place to settle, and my law practice in New Wellington, in addition to ministry with Pastor Templeton, but rest assured, I'll see to all your needs, and you can feel free to approach me anytime with any concerns that you may have."

"Concerns?" Rachel's mind echoed his words, frantically trying to make sense of what Sam was saying.

"That money is rightfully mine to do with as I see fit," she thought. "Pa, when he left me, signed the farm to me and designated Jacob Templeton as guardian over my affairs. I married Ransom and my farm was sold. Oh...when am I to have a say over my own life? Even from the grave, Ransom still has control."

She felt hurt by this new information—and betrayed. For a long moment, she resented Ransom...resented the fact that he never even consulted her about this, never really treated her as an equal, but as though she were some mindless child.

Her conscience struck her like a dart at that thought. No...Ransom always protected her, provided for her, and watched over her. No one had been better to her, except Mother. Nevertheless, he had no right...didn't even talk to her about it...kept his intentions secret from her.

"Sam Spencer...of all people! Sam...who dislikes me and avoids me at every given turn. Why not Tom McClelland? He's an attorney. I like him. Why didn't Ransom choose Tom?"

Sam watched her intently as the struggle within her mirrored on her face. Passivity and aggressiveness wrestled in every fiber of her being. Anger began to build in Rachel like embers being fanned into a roaring blaze, and she felt if she opened her mouth, she would spew red flames of fire. Her huge, dark eyes flashed as her mouth contorted, trying desperately to speak.

"No!" she thought as her stomach began to turn. "This is too much to bear! I could never go to Sam for my needs or even wants, for that matter."

It churned her insides to think she would have to crawl to this man who treated her with such condescension.

Finally, her breath expelled with a loud grunt and she sprang out of her chair, knocking it over. Sam leaped to his feet almost the second she rose.

"How *dare* you, Sam Spencer!" she spat out. "How long did it take you to wangle Ransom into making you executor?"

At her accusation, the blood drained from his tanned face.

"Just what is your *real* intention? Did you think you'd steal my money for yourself?" she continued, with hands on her hips. "Are you so conceited that you would think I'd actually come begging to *you* for money that is rightfully mine?"

"Rachel!" John, taken aback, exclaimed. "You've always been outspoken, but this attack on Sam crosses the line."

White-faced and towering over Rachel, Sam held his hand, palm out, to reason with her, and she attempted to slap it away.

Quickly, his face assumed an air of casual indifference.

His self-possession was an outrage to Rachel and only fanned her indignation.

14

"Don't think for one moment," she rushed on, breathing so hard that she could barely get the words out, "that I need you, *Mr. Spencer*, or anyone else."

She bent over the table and, with one sweep of her hand, sent the documents flying to the earthen floor. The papers landed close to the fire and John, with the tip of his boot, quickly drew them back.

"Let me tell *you* something, Mr. Spencer," Rachel continued, jutting her chin for emphasis, "I can make it on my own...for your information...*if* you're interested, that is."

A vast weariness assailed her, and she swayed dizzily. She suddenly felt faint, and her complexion paled as though she might collapse. John grabbed her, but she feebly shook him off.

She turned to face him and uttered, "And to think that *you*—my own pa—knew about this and didn't say a word to me."

Suddenly, she didn't know who she was most angry with—Sam Spencer or her father.

"Rachel!" Sam's voice came from behind her.

She whirled around and her voice shot like an arrow. "You must both think that I'm some kind of empty-headed fool!"

Blackness was about to overtake her.

"I've got to get out of here before I pass out and disgrace myself," she thought, pressing the back of her hand to her forehead. "Never for one moment must they suspect that just because I'm female, that I'm given to whimpering airs."

Taking a deep breath for strength, and staggering across the room, she pulled open the heavy, log door and slammed it behind her with all the force she could muster. Stumbling to her horse, she wavered a moment, then mounted him, and bending her face into the horse's mane, sped off toward her home called North Star.

Sam ran his fingers through his thick, curly hair as he stared at the papers scattered on the floor. He had anticipated this since the drawing of the will, and had not looked forward to this moment.

"I knew this was going to happen," he said more to himself than to John Winslow. "I told Ransom so. But Ransom wouldn't have it any other way.

"Against my better judgment, I agreed to be executor of her estate," Sam said, clearly frustrated. I want you to know, John, this was not my doing."

"I know that, Sam," John said as he picked up the chair and righted it under the table.

"Ransom knew I couldn't really take care of Rachel. After all, I've got to take the herds to Virginia after they fatten up, and there will be other families from there, no doubt, that will want me to lead them into Kentucky to settle."

Sam collected the will from the floor and shuffled the papers back into order. "He made me promise when he was dying, that I would take care of her, and I am a man who keeps my word."

Shaking his head, he whistled. "Whew! She sure is a handful, that daughter of yours."

John shook his head. "She is that, for sure," he agreed and downed the remainder of his coffee.

Putting a hand on Sam's shoulder, John said, "Listen, Sam…you're just going to have to deal with her the best you can. She's not capable of managing her own affairs, though to hear her tell it, she can conquer just about anything. She's too inexperienced. Ransom knew that. My advice is stand your ground and she'll eventually come around."

Sam nodded doubtfully. "We'll see. But I think there'll be trouble about this for a good while."

When drawing up the will, Sam had argued with Ransom about being executor. Though Sam had ticked off several names that he considered capable, Ransom was adamant. It would be Sam and none other. And when Ransom lay dying on Powell Mountain, he entreated Sam to look after Rachel. Sam solemnly promised to do so, and that was a pledge he would not break, no matter what Rachel put him through.

Though Sam had legal control of Rachel's financial affairs, his heart told him that he no more held sway over her than the man in the moon. Some men, he conceded, would feel intimidated by her temperament.

But not him.

Standing in the middle of the cabin, the more he thought about it, the more he found himself looking forward to their inevitable mental sparring. Seeing her dark eyes turn black with emotion was exhilarating to him—as refreshing as a midsummer's breeze.

No other woman had rattled him like this before. His relationships with women had been escapades that left a trail of broken hearts, sometimes requiring him to enlist the aid of his Congressman father to clean up his untidy messes and smooth things over with the young ladies' families.

Rachel was different. Unpretentious and totally naïve, yet, full of fire, he couldn't charm her as he had others. She intrigued him, and the cat and mouse games he was forced to play with her, whetted his appetite for more. He'd always held the upper hand with women, guarding his heart while trifling with their emotions. But something about Rachel challenged him to stay on the edge, for, like a wild mountain lion, one never knew just which way she would jump.

CHAPTER THREE

RACHEL SLOWED HER HORSE TO A WALK. Tears were coursing down her face and she was nauseated. Across the clearing, she spotted the brook where tangled trees, not yet bare, overhung the water. The cool, clear stream promised a refreshing drink for her upset stomach.

Sliding off her horse, she walked over to the creek on wobbly legs. Crouching over the edge, she scooped water into her hands, drank, and splashed the cool liquid on her face.

She hadn't been feeling well lately. Tiredness seemed to overcome her more quickly, and when working, she often felt the urge to lie down on the spot and sleep. When she finally fell into bed at night, she was asleep before her head hit the pillow—when she wasn't worrying, that is.

"Guess I'm just working too hard," she muttered to herself.

Nestling in the massive tree roots, she brushed the hair from her forehead and mulled over her situation.

Someone was always telling her what to do. Ransom did the same thing, by wanting her to fit in with everyone else in

Wellington. Sit like they did. Talk like they did. Wear the same old stuffy clothes they did. But she couldn't. She wasn't like them.

Her sister-in-law's words rang in her ears for Jane had said on more than one occasion that Rachel was wild. Maybe she was right.

"I can't see wearing a cap or even a hat like they do," she said aloud to the trees. "I like my hair hanging free. And for goodness sake! A *corset* of all things!"

Rachel sighed. She'd tried. Really she had.

"I'll wear a corset when I absolutely have to, but when I'm on my own place, no way!" she thought ruefully. "And I suppose those old biddies will talk about me because I'm not wearing mourning black for Ransom, either. Well, let them!"

Her heart smote her for thinking in such an unkind way. True, some of the women in Wellington had given her a hard time. But, in all honesty, these women who came to Kentucky with her had treated her with a great deal of kindness.

Rachel rubbed her hand over her middle in an effort to still her unsettled stomach. She picked up a twig and chewed on it as she looked across the clearing. Her brow furrowed.

"I can't believe Ransom appointed Sam as executor over my affairs," she said aloud. "Sam Spencer...of all people!"

She didn't understand Sam. He had maintained a distance from her that she found disconcerting. That attitude of cold politeness, and something else in his manner, challenged her to rip off the mask he was wearing.

Sam towered over her, his six feet dwarfing her small frame. His best friend Ransom had been tall, too, but there the similarities stopped. While Ransom had orderly auburn hair, Sam's unruly flame-red hair had tempted her, more than once, to reach out her fingers to put some order to the locks that fell across his forehead.

To her dismay, one time she nearly did.

Common sense began to return her mind to rationality again. There was no way around it. She would just have to deal with Sam the best she could. How on earth would she get him to see her way about things? Suddenly, she sat upright.

"Sure! That's it! Cissa taught me how to flirt! I'll sidle up to him so well that he won't know if he's coming or going."

She slumped back against the tree and frowned. "No, that won't work. Sam isn't a man to be taken in by that kind of behavior. Oh, what a fine dance this will be!"

Rachel drew one knee up, smoothing her skirt carefully to avoid the rip.

A smile tugged at the corners of her mouth as she remembered that night several weeks after she married Ransom. He'd refused to consummate the marriage until he'd had some indication from her that she was ready. When she set out to woo him, it only took about two minutes and he was hooked. That was her sister-in-law Cissa's doing. But it worked.

The corners of her mouth turned down. That worked easily with Ransom, but Sam was a different matter. She'd have to be mighty careful for, word was, he could see right through people.

Frowning, she threw the twig away in annoyance.

"No wonder Pa wouldn't answer my questions about my money these last couple of weeks. I have plans for that money. I want to build that fine, big house that Ransom had planned with quality furnishings. Getting Sam to see it my way will take some doing."

She couldn't help thinking about her dead husband Ransom again. She squeezed her eyes shut as visions of him falling down the mountain onto a precipitous ledge enveloped her, and she tried to block the incident out of her mind. But the sight of him lying there, dying, and his last words to her, "All my love, always" were likely to visit her at any given time.

It had all been very dreamlike since she arrived on her Kentucky land, the passage of days busy with homesteading. Everything she did was with Ransom in mind. How he would have liked this or that done. North Star, the name of their property, was one he had chosen. They had intended to eventually build a large home to house all the children they would have. All she had been able to scurry up for now was her small cabin, but she was determined to eventually build what Ransom had dreamed and planned for, even though his dream of a family would go unfulfilled. She still had the parchment that he had drawn the house on. What rooms would be where.

If it took a lifetime, she would erect what he had envisioned.

She rubbed her hand across her eyes as drowsiness overtook her.

Rachel awoke some time later, feeling groggy, with a mouth that felt like paste. She opened her eyes in confusion and forgot where she was for a few moments.

Looking around, she wondered, "Why am I sitting here in this hot sun?" But the sun had moved and, squinting at the light, she thought, "Why—why it's late afternoon! I must have been asleep for hours."

In spite of her nausea, hunger assaulted her and her growling stomach reminded her that she hadn't eaten since early morning. Glancing where the hackberries overhung the creek, she noted with disappointment the berries were all gone, and remembered their season was over. But she would have liked a little something sweet.

As her mind cleared itself of cobwebs, she recalled the scene that had taken place earlier in Pa's cabin and for an instant regretted ever coming to Kentucky. Regretted meeting a man like Sam! What a fine mess she was in…at the mercy of Sam Spencer!

How he must be laughing at her! The thought of it galled her. Brave words she had spoken back there. Angry words, really. There was nothing like having to eat words spoken in haste, and groveling was not something she was looking forward to.

The thought of bowing and scraping to Sam was enough to make her already nauseous stomach absolutely bilious. Somehow she'll just have to find a way to get around him.

Somehow....

As her mount trotted across the clearing toward home, the sound of a nickering horse sounded behind her. Rising in the saddle and looking around, she saw Sam closing ground toward her.

A groan escaped her lips.

Swinging alongside and slowing his horse to her mount's stride, he said, "Your father's worried about you, Mrs. Templeton."

Rachel only frowned and quickened her horse's pace.

Sam stepped up his horse also. "Did you hear what I said?" There was an edge of something in his voice. Just what, she did not know. Regret, perhaps?

Rachel swallowed a tart reply and rode on in silence, hugging her knees to the horse.

"Rachel?" Sam asked in exasperation as he grabbed the bridle and brought her horse to a stop.

"What?" she protested, as she slapped the reins to no avail.

"Rachel, I don't want you to think that this business about the will was my idea." His tone was apologetic as he tightened his hold on her horse. "It was Ransom's"

"That's a laugh!" she uttered.

"It's important that you realize that," said Sam. "I'll work with you toward your best interests. Believe me, when I say that I don't want to high-hand you."

Rachel said nothing. Not for one moment did she believe that he had no part in Ransom's decision. But just what Sam's reason was, she didn't know. She'd have to think about that for a while. The whole thing puzzled and angered her. She had lost control of her life and it was like a bad taste in her mouth.

She twisted to look at him again and her eyes widened when she caught a look in his eyes that made her breathing freeze. It was that same look of unabashed admiration that brought heat to her cheeks the first time she saw him at the livery in Wellington, Virginia, several months ago.

Her face flushed and her eyes flickered away from the intensity of his gaze.

"If you'll ride over to my place, we can discuss it in more detail," he told her matter-of-factly.

When she looked at him again, his face was wiped clean of any emotion. Had she been mistaken?

Though yearning was no longer on his face, there was something in his voice that made her feel vulnerable. Something…her intuition warned her to guard against.

"Sorry," she said a little stiffly. "I've got to get on home." Rachel tried to jerk the reins from his grasp.

"Let go!" she cried, and suddenly the nausea she'd been fighting all morning besieged her. The hot afternoon sun spun revoltingly for a few moments, and as she leaned against the mane of her horse, her stomach finally heaved up the remains of her breakfast.

Rising afterward, Rachel reluctantly accepted the handkerchief Sam passed her and wiped her mouth. Mortified, her head dropped. Vomited! And that he, of all people, should see her in this state!

"Have you been ill, Rachel?" Sam asked, concerned. "Is there anything—"

Her head rose again and her face was pale, but on it was determination to somehow reclaim her dignity and go home.

"It's nothing for you to be concerned about," she told Sam. "I'm fine."

He looked as though he did not believe her and opened his mouth to comment to that effect.

Instead, he said, "I'll see you home, then."

"Thank you, no," she replied. With a final jerk, the reins were free.

"I can take care of myself," she said as she threw his handkerchief at him.

"Great!" she thought as she sped away. "His first attempt to settle this and I messed it up. I'm not getting off to a very good start. But something about that man riles me past reason. Rachel, old girl, you'd better get a grip on your emotions and handle this in a different way."

A loud rumble of an empty stomach made her forget her dilemma for the moment. "I'll think about this later," she said aloud. "Maybe Louise has some leftovers from lunch."

CHAPTER FOUR

IT HAD BEEN MORE THAN TWO MONTHS since Rachel had been to New Wellington. As she entered the town, a newly erected sign read, "Population 223".

She looked about in amazement, for the span of untamed country she remembered seeing when they arrived, was gone. Despite all that Frank had told her about the town, she never visualized what was before her now. The town she saw sprawling around her was unfamiliar. Gone were the massive trees that had shrouded the landscape in darkness.

New Wellington, in all its primitive beginnings, was becoming an expansive force ever pushing against its boundaries.

She marveled at all the new construction. Families were bunking together in hastily assembled cabins while their large homes were feverishly being erected. Will Templeton's saw mill equipment had arrived from Virginia, and Will was running it day and night to furnish lumber for the homes and businesses the citizens were zealously trying to get built before winter set in.

The driving excitement of the town was contagious. The sight of so many people hurrying about made Rachel, fresh from the quiet of her farm, conscious of her heart quickening in step to the bustle around her.

Narrow, hard-packed, earthen side streets, designated for residential housing, turned off the wide expanse of Main Street, and the noise of hammers striking was constant, long after folks were in bed, tugging and transforming a wilderness into a semblance of settled and tamed terrain.

Already the street was crowded with businesses selling wares shipped down the Ohio.

Walkways in front of the merchants' buildings were not completed yet, except for a few stretches here and there.

Rachel had been so engrossed in her own part of this new world, getting her own estate into some appearance of estate life, she hadn't given a thought to the fact that these hardy people she had traveled from Virginia with were meeting the same challenges she was, conquering the wilderness and bending nature to their plans and schemes. All that was familiar now were the people as they moved quickly about the settlement.

New Wellington was named for the town of Wellington in Virginia, where they had moved from. But as fascinating as these industrious people were, and the changes they were making here, town life was not for her. She grew up in the country and city life stifled her. Living with the Templeton family in Wellington had revealed that soon enough.

Her visit to town was not just a matter of curiosity. Rachel had been feeling under the weather for quite some time, and Louise had talked her into seeing Doctor Stone.

"Probably just has to do with Ransom's passing," Louise had offered. "Perhaps the doctor has a tonic to perk you up."

She'd been meaning to come to town sooner. A wagon was something she definitely needed. The few times Frank had been to town for meal and flour and other staples, had proved difficult as he had to transport it home on packhorses, leaving her temporarily without animals to haul away brush.

She was grateful that her brother-in-law Will Templeton had delivered all her belongings and the few pieces of furniture she had owned in Wellington. Most of it was still packed in crates as the cabin barely accommodated Frank, Louise, and herself.

A large house was what she had been thinking about…Ransom's house…his plans. It was vital that she become self-sufficient to prove to Sam that she didn't need him.

But first things first. She definitely needed that wagon.

"Land sakes, Rachel, is that you?" Gerald Miller cried when he saw her.

Rachel stopped and slid down from her horse.

"You haven't been to town in weeks. I was just saying to Martha the other day, 'I wonder how Rachel is?' I'm mighty sorry about Ransom, him being killed like that. You know he was like a son to me. You'd have to go far to find as fine a man as he was."

"Thank you, Mr. Miller," she murmured. The first surge of excitement upon entering New Wellington had faded, and suddenly she began to wish she had not ventured to town. Tears smarted in the back of her eyes.

"I'd known him all his life," Gerald continued. "Thought the world of him, I did. If anyone had godly character, Ransom did."

"Please, Mr. Miller," she said, casting her eyes down. "I don't wish to talk about it."

He colored slightly. "Sorry, Rachel, of course—I understand."

Her eyes scanned the town. "Could you tell me where to find Doctor Stone?"

"Of course," he answered, pointing his finger. "Just head towards the center of town, right where they're going to put the courthouse. His building is on the right, two streets down. Can't miss it."

She was stopped repeatedly by people she had come to New Wellington with. Some she knew slightly, but practically everyone she met mentioned Ransom. If she heard one more person bring up his name she would scream.

She mustn't cry. Not now. Not until she was safely on the way home. She must think of something else to talk about, but it was hard, for Ransom had been a favorite with the people.

"Rachel!"

Rachel stopped, turned, and spotting red hair under an angled parasol, saw Abigail Newgate hurrying towards her. Abigail, and her father Cabot Newgate, had been waiting to join their party at the Anderson Blockhouse in Virginia when they arrived at that milestone on their journey.

Then, two men had showed up from Charleston, South Carolina and arrested Cabot for theft back in that city. With Abigail left on her own, Gabe Roswell, another member of the party, took care of Abigail at her father's request and they had progressed into an 'understanding'.

"Rachel!" Abigail cried again. "I haven't seen you since we arrived. How have you been?"

"Oh, I've been busy. You know how it is, making a new start somewhere. How about yourself? Are you teaching school yet?"

"Oh, yes! I absolutely love it! I have twenty-three students. Pastor Templeton says that he would like to start another school at Mission Point sometime in the future and asked if I'd be willing to teach there also."

Abigail's face lit with an infectious smile. "I suppose you've heard that Gabe and I are engaged?"

Rachel smiled back, remembering that Frank had told her the news after one of his trips to town, but she hadn't paid much attention to him.

Ransom's mother Elizabeth had been in a tizzy, according to Frank, wanting to coordinate the first wedding in New Wellington. Always the perfect hostess, everyone sought Elizabeth's advice on matters of etiquette and she readily gave it.

Originally referring to Gabe Roswell as Old Testament Elijah the Tishbite, she was pleased that she had managed to turn him into a respectable, if somewhat coarse, gentleman.

"Yes. I heard something about it, Abigail. Do you have any immediate plans for the wedding?"

"Not just yet. Gabe has settled on some land outside New Wellington. He's living in a cabin for the present but he's building a house for us. You know him," she said with a roll of her eyes. "Not exactly a town dweller."

Rachel laughed and shrugged one shoulder. "Well—yes. I can relate to that. I don't care much for settlement living myself."

"I'd say the wedding will take place in a few months, maybe sometime in the spring. You're invited. You know that, don't you?"

Rachel shook her head. "Of course, Abigail. I'll try my best to be there."

"Good. I'm just on my way home. Would you like to come with me and visit for a while?"

"No, thank you," Rachel responded and was already moving away. "I haven't been feeling well and I'm trying to find Doctor Stone."

"Oh, he's easy to find," Abigail pointed, "right up the street. You'll see his sign."

"Thanks," said Rachel, preparing to walk away.

"By the way, Rachel," Abigail dropped her voice a notch and placed her hand on Rachel's arm, "I'm so sorry for what happened to Ransom," she said sympathetically. "I know you must be taking it very hard. If there's anything I can do, anything at all, just let me know."

Rachel looked at Abigail and smiled…a quiet and simple smile of gratitude. "Thank you, Abigail, but I'll be just fine," she assured her." I really must go now."

"Of course," she replied and removed her hand. "Look me up, Rachel, anytime you come to town."

Hoping there wouldn't be questions from anyone else, Rachel walked on until she spied the doctor's sign on the other side. She crossed over, holding her skirts up a little to keep them from the dust, passed the horses tied to the hitching rail, tied her own horse alongside them, and stepped onto the boardwalk in front of Burnett's Dress Shop.

She spotted a bonnet in the tiny window and stopped. She didn't especially like hats, but she planned to see Sam today. Touching her loose tresses, she instantly regretted coming to town without doing anything more than run a comb through them. The least she could have done was to pin them back.

Sighing, she opened the door and walked inside, immediately noticing a dress that, at first, made her a little uncomfortable with its lack of flaring skirt. Looking it over closely, she saw that it was an informal style, with a high waist and the skirt hanging close to the body.

Cocking her head to one side, she decided, yes…this was a dress that was more to her liking. In fact, it fitted her style perfectly. She hated corsets and there was no need to wear one with this dress. It had more of a natural look to it.

Rachel wondered if it was the latest style and what the other ladies thought of such attire. There had been nothing like this back in Wellington. She would be sure to ask Elizabeth for she would know, even in this wild part of the country, what was in style. She had connections in Virginia that kept in contact by post, and Rachel wondered if this dress had been made at Elizabeth's urging.

Tearing her eyes away from the dress, she glanced at the bonnet in the window. As much as she needed something to cover her hair, she had no money. Ruth Burnett was assisting another lady with a bolt of cloth, but Rachel took a step towards her and opened her mouth to ask for credit.

Ruth turned, smiled pleasantly, and asked, "Is there something I can help you with, Rachel?"

Rachel stopped, smiled weakly, spread her hands, and said, "No—no, ma'am. Forget it."

She walked out, embarrassed, and thoroughly frustrated by her financial situation.

CHAPTER FIVE

RACHEL WALKED NEXT DOOR TO THE DOCTOR'S OFFICE. His building was one of the first to be constructed in town, she'd been told.

The door opened with a creak and she quickly stepped inside, expecting to see Doctor Stone.

But in walked James Templeton, her brother-in-law, from the back room.

"James!" she cried with happiness. "What are you doing in Doctor Stone's office?"

"Rachel!" He colored with pleasure at her delight in seeing him again. He took her hands in his and his shy manner disappeared as he beamed and exclaimed with pride, "I'm working with Doctor Stone. I'm training to be a doctor."

"You are, James?" she exclaimed, wide-eyed. "Really? A doctor?"

"Yes, I am. It's something I've been thinking about for quite a while."

"But...I thought you were going to be in ministry with your father."

"Oh, I am…I am. I think both will work together. Ministry for the soul and medicine for the body," he smiled as released her hands and hooked his thumbs in his trousers.

"Well, that's just fine, James. I'm so happy for you. Oh! You must tell me! How are the family and Cissa?"

"She's fine and wondering how you are. She's been pestering me to bring her to your place. You know she's with child."

"Yes, I know. I'll try to look her up before I leave today."

James was her favorite of Ransom's two brothers. So sweet and unruffled in temperament, he would make a good doctor. Cissa had a good husband…that was for sure.

"Well, Rachel," Doctor Stone informed her as he helped her to sit up on the table, "it seems as though you are nearly four months pregnant. The baby should be here about the last of March or first of April next year."

She was stunned.

Pregnant! With Ransom's baby! Mentally, she began to tick back the time. It should have been easy for her to guess, but she had been so busy on the farm.

A baby! After she got over her shock she warmed to his diagnosis. Though Ransom was dead, a part of him would live on at North Star.

Then, frowning, she remembered back to this past spring. She had delivered another child. However, the baby hadn't lived. The thought frightened her, and in a hushed whisper, she told Doctor Stone so.

"I'd wondered what had happened to the baby, Rachel. You stuck yourself out on that farm in Virginia. As I recall your baby was due in July, was it not?"

"Y—yes," she stammered. "I went into labor early. Ransom was home from the university and he came to my farm and found me in labor. He delivered the baby. She was...."

"Stillborn?" he questioned.

She dropped her head slightly. "Yes," she answered dully. Raising her head, she said, "Please...please don't say anything about that to anyone, Doctor Stone. No one knows that I was pregnant."

Doctor Stone studied her, thoughtful. Strange, that she wanted no one to discover her previous pregnancy. Of course, being with child in her first marriage to a notorious gambler might have something to do with that.

"Don't worry, Rachel. You have my word. I won't." He turned to wash his hands in the basin on a small stand near the examination table, and sternly advised, "But I want to see you more often so I can monitor this pregnancy."

A cold little fear was beginning to throb in Rachel's throat as memories of that tragic birth filled her heart. Through stiff lips she asked, "Is there something wrong?" When he didn't answer immediately, "You must tell me, Doctor!" she begged. "Will the baby be all right?"

The doctor immediately regretted his sternness, and he clucked his tongue softly as he dried his hands with a towel. "We certainly hope that everything will be fine. However...."

Fear stabbed Rachel's heart again.

"Because your first pregnancy ended in a stillborn birth, I'd like—just for precaution's sake, mind you—to see you at least once a month. I know you're industrious, Rachel, and have a lot to do in settling your place. Nevertheless, in light of the circumstances, you need to take it easy until this child is born."

Rachel stepped out of Doctor Stone's office with worry firmly entrenched in her mind. "It would be an easier day," Rachel thought as she headed down the walk, "if only Mother could be here." It had been so long since she last saw her.

It came as a surprise that she hadn't thought of Mother in days and with that knowledge came a sense of guilt. Since her mother had died two years ago, she had thought of her every day until the past few weeks. The matter of living and surviving weighed heavily upon her. She missed the carefree days of childhood. Days that were free from worry…free from thoughts about survival…crops, her herds, and the fences to be built.

Oh, Mother, I miss you so. Her childhood really wasn't so long ago, but in her seventeenth year now, she felt as if she had lived a lifetime.

Not paying heed to where she was walking, she collided into Will Templeton and he reached out to steady her.

"Rachel! Where have you been?" he asked. "The family's been wondering about you. You haven't been to Sunday church for a while."

"Will! I'm so glad to see you!" she exclaimed. "I know I've been a bad girl, not coming to church," she admitted guiltily. "It's just that I've been so busy with the farm and all. Please tell Jacob and Elizabeth that I miss them, and I promise I'll start coming to the services soon."

"Good!" he answered. "Are you getting along all right? I was going to try to find some time to come out and check on you. But, to tell you the truth, I've been working so hard, I do well just to make it home at times."

Rachel warmed to his concern. Memories of staying with his family for a year flitted across her mind, and she suddenly realized she yearned for them all terribly. She hungered for the comforting inspiration of Jacob Templeton and the warm love of his wife, Elizabeth. Rachel missed her own mother, needed her right now, and if she could just get to Elizabeth and lay her head on her breast, some of the anxiety might leave her.

"I came into town to see Doctor Stone," she hesitantly offered.

Will examined her face closely. "Are you sick, Rachel? You *are* rather pale."

Rachel looked at Will and smiled. "No. Not sick, Will. Well, yes…but not really."

He looked at her confused. Dropping her head and twiddling her fingers, "I—I just want you to know that I'm having a child," she blurted out, "Ransom's child."

He stood still for a moment. His youngest brother was dead, and Mother and Father still in intense grief. And now to find out that Ransom's widow was pregnant with his child.

In his usual whirlwind fashion, Will grabbed Rachel by the waist, lifted her up in the air, and whirled her around, much to the surprise and disapproval of the residents milling in the street.

A gentleman did not exhibit such behavior in public, and the fact that it was his sister-in-law made it scandalous.

Rachel laughed at his impetuous action. That was exactly what she needed.

Setting her down with a smile covering his whole face, Will tipped back his hat and exclaimed, "Well—well—well. Ransom's child! Now, what do you know about that!"

"Oh, my!" Rachel said, pressing her palms together in front of her as it dawned on her what she had just done. She had told Will in public, and of all places, on Main Street of New Wellington, and now everyone would know. And what Elizabeth will say about all this when she hears—well, she was such a stickler for decorum.

"Mother and Father will have to be told," Will offered, ignoring her embarrassment. "You know that, don't you, Rachel?" A small cloud passed over his face. "Mother is still grieving so over Ransom."

Taking her hands in his, he said, "I think knowing you're carrying his son will help her immensely."

"How do you know it will be a son?"

"Of course, it will be a son," he confidently answered.

She laughed again.

"How soon?" he questioned.

"Doctor Stone says about the last of March or first of April."

"Um. Well, keep us informed about what's going on." He drew his eyebrows together. "Now don't you stay stuck out on that farm of yours without letting us know anything."

"I promise, Will."

Releasing her hands, he repositioned his hat.

"Listen, Rachel, I've got to run," he said, in a hurry as usual. "As you can see," he looked around and swept his hand through the air, "it's absolutely crazy right now with all the building going on. If you need anything—anything at all—just let me know. My house is the last on the left at the end of this street. I'll do my best to help you any way I can."

Will put his finger under Rachel's chin and forced her face up. "Now promise me that you will come to me. Do I have your word on that?"

She shook her head yes and smiled. "I promise."

He kissed her quickly on the forehead. "I'm sorry I've got to leave you, but I've been busy day and night with the sawmill. We miss you, you know."

"Miss you, too. And Will—" she said warmly, "thanks a lot."

"Sure thing," he answered and hurried away.

She liked Will, even though he could be terribly direct at times. But still, you knew where you stood with him. He was a man known to keep his word and to have excellent business sense, and others looked up to him and valued his opinion.

CHAPTER SIX

RACHEL WALKED TO WHERE THE COURTHOUSE was to be erected, right in the middle of the square. Sam had built his office, adjoining Tom's, on the corner of Main and Willow Streets.

Her steps slowed and she stood in the street, looking at the sign that read, "Sam Spencer, Attorney at Law," debating whether to go in. She wasn't sure she was in the frame of mind to transact any business with Sam, and perhaps he wasn't in his office anyway.

She nearly turned to walk away, but they needed more provisions at the farm. The last thing she wanted to do was to negotiate with him, but they were running dangerously low.

And there was the matter of the wagon she desperately needed. In addition, if she got her way, she'd leave today with Sam's permission for lumber to build her house.

Taking a deep breath, she walked to the entrance and, hiking up her skirts, climbed the temporary stoop and opened the door.

As she closed it behind her, a murmuring of voices from the other room halted and Sam appeared in the office doorway.

"Rachel!" he acknowledged warmly as he walked toward her.

She gave a slight nod and spoke stiffly. "Mr. Spencer."

He stopped at the cool tone in her voice.

Resuming his stride, he pulled a chair out for her. "Please sit down," he said. "I won't be long."

Sam disappeared into the other room. Behind the closed door, soft feminine laughter was heard, and Rachel cocked her head, straining to recognize the voice.

After a few moments, she shrugged her shoulders as her surroundings captured her attention. "A narrow building," she noted. "A little rough for Sam," she thought. "After all, he's used to luxury. Sam has traveled in the best circles since his father is a Congressman." She frowned. "Or so Ransom told me."

She crossed her legs and swung her foot aimlessly. "I don't understand why someone like him wants to come to this wilderness. Maybe that's why he looks down on me. Probably thinks I'm just some wild country girl." She almost giggled. "Well, come to think of it, I guess I am."

She uncrossed her legs and sat upright, gathering an air of respectability about her. She tossed her head slightly without realizing she had done so. "Still, that's no reason to look down on me."

Her indignant reverie was broken when the office door opened and Sam escorted a tall blonde into the waiting area. She was at least five feet, eight inches tall, with creamy skin that glowed, and the gaze she gave Sam was not just the look of a client. Her pale-green muslin dress with yellow trim accentuated her sparkling green eyes fixed firmly on Sam.

Sam put his arm across the girl's shoulder and leaned toward her murmuring, eliciting the girl's silky laughter as though sharing a private joke.

That was something Elizabeth would say a gentleman should not do.

Rachel grew tense, sitting there, glaring at them both. She tried to keep her eyes from those two, but found it difficult to do.

Looking down at her own outfit, she realized she had come to town so hurriedly that she'd given no thought to her attire. Her dress revealed her lack of expertise in her attempts to mend several places that had torn while working the land.

Louise was an expert seamstress, but she had her hands full with other domestic duties as the fruit had been ripening, ready for preserving.

While in Virginia, the Templeton women had tried their best to teach her the skills that all respectable women of the day should know. Those talents were proudly displayed by Wellington ladies at their monthly sewing circles, but Rachel had hated the meetings, which seemed to her nothing more than an opportunity for gossip, and most of it quite escaped her anyway. But as she was a ward of the Templeton family, she was expected to graciously attend even though it soon became obvious to the members, she would never learn.

Her mother had made an attempt to instruct her in cooking and sewing as well, but the call of the outdoors made her an unwilling pupil. And as her father John preferred Rachel to be the wild, unself-conscious creature that he enjoyed roaming the woods and fields with, Emily ceased her gentle persuasions, reasoning there would be time when Rachel was older.

As a result, Rachel thought nothing of sewing uneven stitches in her half-hearted attempts to rescue a torn frock at the end of a long, tiresome day. After all, it didn't matter what the dress looked like. She saw very few people, and those she did see were overwhelmed with their own duties.

Suddenly, she resented the girl with the soft, throaty laugh, dressed in fashionable clothes…resented the fact that she seemed to hold some type of feminine power over Sam Spencer. Rachel's nails dug into the palms of her hands as she felt an odd pang. Sam meant nothing to her, she rationalized, but the sting she felt would not go away. This feeling was foreign to her and she wasn't quite sure how to handle it.

"Well," began Sam as he closed the door. He was in a good mood, almost jovial, in fact. It didn't take much, even for Rachel as naïve as she was, to imagine what put him in that frame of mind. He slapped his hands together.

"Just what can I do for you today, Rachel?"

Rachel was dying to ask Sam who the pretty girl was. She certainly hadn't been on the caravan with them. Was she perhaps someone he knew from Philadelphia? They were too familiar to be strangers, she surmised. No man would take such liberties with a lady, familiar or not.

"But this is Sam," she reasoned, "with the reputation of a ladies' man."

She dug her nails into the palms of her hands again. "I—I need to talk to you about...." She flushed as the heat rose in her cheeks. Rachel glanced at the door and it beckoned her to slip out the way she came.

"Yes?" Sam asked—his eyes sharp with interest.

She hesitated, then drew herself up to her fullest and exclaimed, "Money."

A look of devilment appeared in his eyes and she could have kicked herself. She had given a lot of thought all morning what she would say, and the words she had rehearsed evaporated in her agitation. She felt herself fidgeting and tried to stop.

Why does Sam make me lose all composure?

"Come into my office," he motioned, interrupting her thoughts.

Following the direction of his sweeping hand, she walked in and took her place in the chair opposite his desk. She glanced sideways at Sam as he gathered the documents in front of him and placed them to the side. He was impeccably dressed while she looked…well…like a field hand.

Well, that's exactly what I've been doing.

Her hands began to sweat and, as she looked down at them, became painfully aware of the state her nails were in. Goodness! They were broken and irregular. Dirt beneath her nails, of all things! Her mended dress, though clean, was not one she should have worn to town, and her hair cascaded down her back in an unruly way. She knew she must look as disorderly as she felt.

Rachel swallowed hard. Here she was coming to Sam looking like a pauper, when she should have been dressed like a queen granting favors. How did she expect him to give her what she really wanted?

Oh why didn't I wear one of my better dresses! Goodness knows I've got plenty!

Elizabeth had seen to that in Virginia.

She wavered between bolting from the office and staying.

"What exactly do you need the money for, Rachel?" he asked, right to the point.

Her head shot up and she saw the twinkle in his eyes. Sam was enjoying this too much…way too much.

"I need some provisions for the farm."

"Such as?"

"Um…you know flour Things like that." She looked down again and fingered the mended folds of her dress. "And I also need to buy a wagon," she added.

43

"Oh. Well, that's easily taken care of," he casually stated. "There's already an account at Templeton Store for you. You should know that already."

Rachel hadn't given much thought to how Frank had purchased supplies in the past. She didn't really think to ask.

"We'll go over to Cromwell's to purchase a wagon."

He picked up a ledger that read, *Accounts, Rachel Templeton* and proceeded to write. She was nervous. How could she ask him for money to purchase lumber for her new house? The temptation to snatch the ledger from his hand was almost too much to bear. That was her money and she should have the say-so over it.

That thought was enough to spur her on.

Looking up, he asked, "Anything else?" with suspicion growing on his face.

Her eyes darted from his hands to her own. How did he keep his hands so groomed when she knew he worked as hard as anyone else? They were remarkably well tended for someone who spent time clearing his own property and herding cattle. They were perfect hands, except for a few tiny scars. Scars: the result of a cyclone that had struck them on the journey here.

Her mind drifted back to that incident when she had been hurled about by the wind and tangled in thorny brush. Heedless of cuts and lacerations, his bleeding hands had rescued her that day. She remembered too, his cries of concern, so uncharacteristic of him, as he cried out to God, pleading that she still be alive. Those things burned in her memory and she would never forget them until the day she died.

"Rachel?"

She cleared her throat and squared her shoulders. "Well...yes," she said, trying her best to sound businesslike. "I do have another request. I would like to buy some lumber."

"Lumber?"

"Yes, that's right."

Sam frowned slightly. "Whatever for? You have an ample cabin."

This was not going well at all. His bluntness ruined all hopes of leading up to the matter in any persuasive way. She wished, in that moment, that she had not mentioned it. Drawing a deep breath, she looked frantically around the room, longing to disappear. "Well...."

"Yes?" he asked, waiting.

She rushed on, "I'd like to begin construction on a new house."

"A new house?" he incredulously asked, looking at her as though she had lost her mind.

"Yes," she declared with a decided edge to her voice.

His voice was sharp. "Don't you think you have enough to do right now without worrying about building a new house?"

Rachel had expected this reaction and she turned to Sam with eyes that had darkened to black, eyes ready to do battle.

"Well, just look at all the folks in town," she reasoned, swiping a hand in the air. "They're all putting up new houses. I think I have the right to do the same."

"What the folks do in town," Sam explained patiently, "has nothing to do with North Star. The people in town are not clearing a vast acreage of land and tending a herd of cattle. You are. And the only help you have is Frank, and he can't handle everything."

"Are you saying you won't give me the money?" her voice raising a notch.

He raised his hands, palms out. "Don't get defensive, Rachel. I'm only trying to have a sensible conversation. Building a new home is not a priority right now."

Lowering his hands and locking the fingers together, he continued, "I'm just saying that now is not the time to take on such a responsibility. Winter will soon be here, and if you don't mind my saying it," glancing at her face, "you're not looking any too well, either."

"I do mind!" she cried as she jumped to her feet. Sam shoved his chair back and was immediately on his feet as well.

A wave of sickness swept over her. She stood there for a moment and gradually the feeling began to subside. In a minute she'd feel all right and, then with all the poise she could muster, she would leave his office.

She composed her face into more tranquil lines. Knowing she must look like a wild mustang, she pushed back the hair that had fallen over her face. She would give several gold coins right now for the egrettes Elizabeth had given her...that is, *if* she had her money.

Sam watched her with intensity, brows drawn, waiting to hear what she would say next.

What a fool she had been to think she could get what she wanted just for the asking! Especially the way she looked! It would have been difficult enough even if she had worn one of her prettiest frocks. But as tacky as he must think she appeared, it was impossible, especially since he had just been with that other lady. She knew his reputation with women. She must have been delirious to think she could compete with them or anyone else, for that matter. Oh! What a fool!

In the heat of rejection, her temper began to rise again.

With a defiant look on her face, she lifted her chin and asked, "Are you telling me no?"

"Don't act childish, Rachel," he spoke as his eyebrows drew together again. "It's only for now."

"Fine," she spat out as she turned to go.

"I'll come with you to buy that wagon," he calmly suggested as he grabbed his hat.

"Suit yourself," she threw over her shoulder as she rushed toward the door.

She stepped outside so quickly that she forgot there was no boardwalk. She stumbled and would have fallen headfirst, had Sam not seized her shoulders.

Shrugging him off was no easy task, for he refused to let go of her arm as she started to cross the street.

"Calm down, Rachel. People will start talking. Although, I don't care myself, I know it would bother you immensely."

She pushed her wavy, black mane into some semblance of order.

"This will never happen again! I'll look my best next time I come to see Sam!"

A part of her instantly deflated. "Of course, looking my best won't be possible for too much longer with this baby coming."

CHAPTER SEVEN

SAM LEFT CROMWELL'S WAGON SHOP and was walking back to his office when he heard his name called. He turned and saw Will quickly stepping toward him.

"Sorry, I couldn't be there today, Sam. How did the meeting go with the town council?"

"I think we got some important issues resolved," said Sam. "The council decided to build the courthouse out of brick instead of wood, particularly since fire is such a hazard. And it looks like the whole town is filling up with new business. You know...next year, instead of importing in basics like meal and flour from Logan County, we should grind our own here."

"Way ahead of you there," Will said to Sam. "I'm planning on building a mill on Ezzel Creek. I've also been tossing the idea around of going to Logan County to buy some pigs. Hogs would be a good sell to the East."

"Hmm. You're right about that. Let me know when you're ready to go and I'll go with you. They don't call it 'Rogues' Harbour' for nothing, you know. It's a rough county, I've heard, and it wouldn't hurt to take a couple of other men with us. You know the old adage, 'there's safety in numbers'.

"My problem is, that I don't have the help for my farm and I've been kicking around the idea of buying some indentured servants back East and bringing them here.

"Rachel needs more help for her place, too, and...by the way...did you know that Ransom willed me as power of attorney over her estate until she's twenty-five?"

Will tossed Sam a thoughtful look. "No, I didn't, Sam. I've been so busy myself. How's that working out?"

Sam rubbed his chin and laughed. "It's challenging to say the least."

Will echoed his laugh. "Well, we all know how headstrong Rachel is. But, she's a good girl. Say...did you know she's expecting Ransom's child?"

A baby! It took several seconds for that to sink in. So that's why Rachel looked under the weather! And why she'd been sick. He'd noticed the dark circles under her eyes and wondered if she'd been working too hard.

"I can see by your expression that you didn't," Will remarked. "She just found out today from Doc Stone. Due sometime about March or April, I think she said. I'm glad she has Frank and Louise out there with her. The way things are booming, I don't have any time at all to look in on her, myself. I just hope she doesn't overwork herself. We don't want anything to happen to my little brother's baby."

"The little simpleton!" Sam thought. "Wanting to take on raising a house in her condition! I'll have to get things wrapped up so I can go back East. Yes. Indentured servants are the answer. I'm sure of it!"

"Let me know," Will continued, "when you leave for Virginia. There are provisions you can pick up for me and ship down the Ohio."

Sam rode over to Rachel's place a couple of weeks later. It was a warm November morning and Rachel was busy milking in the small barn Frank and John had raised.

Sam opened the gate and walked through the brush corral that Frank had thrown up for the horses.

Rachel was wearing a pair of britches and her hair was tied back with a piece of twang leather. Her waist was thickening slightly and she had on one of Ransom's too-large shirts that hung to her knees.

"Hello, Rachel."

Rachel jumped at the sound of a voice and saw it was Sam. He'd been as quiet as an Indian. Of all times for him to drop by! Her looking a mess as usual!

As she rose from the stool, a wave of dizziness swept over her. Sam quickly reached her side. "Steady, Rachel," he said, a firm hold on her arm.

Rachel nodded and in a few seconds moved away from him.

"Well?" she bristled as she pushed up the sleeves of the shirt. "Aren't you going to say something about my pants? Nearly everyone else has had a say about them!" As soon as the words were out of her mouth, she wished she could take them back.

Sam raised his eyebrows and rubbed his finger over the bridge of his nose. "What makes you think I care if you wear britches?"

"It's—it's just that people gave me a hard time about it in Virginia," she remarked defensively.

"Well this is *New* Wellington, Kentucky, not Wellington, Virginia," he countered. "And if you're set on wearing them, then, at least, get that chip off your shoulder."

"I don't have a chip on my shoulder," she denied.

He pushed his hat back, put his hands on his hips, and laughed. "Little lady, I don't think there's anyone around who's got a chip bigger than you. Do what you want. If you want to wear trousers, then wear them. But be prepared to expect a backlash of gossip if you go against society. Remember…like it or not, society has a hard time swallowing the fact that someone is different. And being different can bring loneliness."

She thought about that for a moment. She'd had Mother and Pa while growing up in isolation, and had never felt lonely. Only after Mother died and Pa left her to the Templeton family, did she feel lonely. Of course, she had Ransom as her friend, but still, she had never fit in with the towns-people, never really wanted to. No, she never felt lonely when alone. "Only with others," she thought in bewilderment.

She shut her eyes hard, blocking out the confusing thoughts Sam had presented. Opening them and casting him a glance, she reasoned, "I only wear them on the farm."

"That's *your* business."   Sam shrugged his shoulders. "Truthfully, it makes no difference to me whether you wear them or not."

Apparently.

"What did you come out here for, anyway?" she clipped brusquely as she moved the stool out of the cow's way.

"Merely business, I assure you."

She looked up expectantly.

"And?"

He shifted his stance. "I'm setting my affairs in order. I'll be leaving for the East to buy some indentured servants for my place. After tossing the idea around, I thought that would be the best solution for your place, also."

"Inden—what?"

"Indentured servants. Usually, those coming to this country and don't have money for passage on the ship. They sell themselves for service, for say...um...seven years. You could use the help now that...."

She raised her eyebrows. "Now that, what?" she asked.

He folded his arms as a look she couldn't define passed over his face. "Why didn't you tell me you were going to have a baby?"

Her eyes opened wide in surprise and her cheeks pinked with embarrassment.

"How did you—?" she finally sputtered.

"Never mind," he interrupted, giving her a nod. "I found out. I make it my business to keep up to date about you."

Rachel's forehead puckered. "Because of your promise to Ransom, I suppose."

"Partly."

She opened her mouth to ask about the other part, but Sam quickly cut her off.

"Now that the subject of your pregnancy has been brought up," he said as he unfolded his arms, "I have some advice that I sincerely wish you would take. I'd like for you to stay with Jacob and Elizabeth Templeton while I'm gone."

"Whatever for?" she asked in amazement. "You know I don't like living in town. With all the crowds there, town life would absolutely stifle me. Besides," she reasoned, "I have too much work to do here."

"My point, exactly. You need to take it easy now. After all, you must take special care...."

She narrowed her eyes at him. "For what?"

"Your baby, that's, for what."

Shrugging one shoulder, she said, "I have Louise."

"As though Louise or anyone else could convince you to slow down," he countered cynically. "Consider the child, Rachel."

Fear swept over her face. "Did anyone tell—?"

Sam studied her for a moment. "What did Doctor Stone say to you, Rachel?"

She turned from him. She didn't like anyone knowing her troubles, especially Sam. It was enough that he was involved in and controlled her business affairs. She could do without his concern in the rest of her life.

Taking hold of her forearm, he asked quietly, "Answer me, Rachel. What did the doctor tell you?"

She tried in vain to shake off his hand. His hold tightened. "Tell me!"

"All right!" she said through gritted teeth. "He has some concerns about the baby and wants me to see him at least once a month, that's all."

Sam grew quiet. "Are you going to take his advice?" he finally asked.

She snapped, "Of course, I am, if it's any of your business."

"I'll hold you to that," he said as he released her arm. "I don't want to worry about you while I'm gone."

"That's a laugh," she thought, "Sam Spencer worrying about me."

Anxious to change the subject, she asked, "When will you return?"

"I hope to be back by the last of January." Rubbing his chin, he added, "The end of February at the latest."

"So soon?"

"I'm not going the road. I'll be traveling the Ohio River."

"Oh," she said for want of anything better to say. She'd heard the men talk about the treachery of traveling the Ohio. "Easy pickings" they had said, with Indians hiding on the banks and attacking the boats as they went by. Thank goodness, the goods of the people she'd traveled here with had arrived safely at the Falls of the Ohio. Still...she wondered if the road would be a better way for Sam to travel.

He cut into her thoughts. "Anything you want me to get for you while I'm gone?"

"Wha—?" She gave her head a little shake. With a frown etching her forehead, she asked, "Sam....do you think the Ohio's the way you should go? I've heard—"

"I know what you've heard," he informed her. "But I'll take my chances and believe that God is with me."

She scowled. "That may be, but...."

He leaned in ever so slightly, and she could almost feel his breath warm against her hair. His blue eyes were alert, searching her face. He caught her gaze. "Is this concern I hear, Rachel? Does it matter so much to you?" he asked her, that baiting quality in his voice echoing his past triumphant romantic pursuits.

Speechless, she was confused at the feeling that swept over her. She stared at his mouth and wondered what it would be like to kiss him. She looked into his eyes and Sam's eyes darkened as he read the message hers conveyed. Her heartbeat quickened as her stomach began to somersault.

"Well...does it?" he said with quiet urgency.

Her lips parted as her eyes grew wider. In that instant the cow knocked over the pail and the spell was broken. Sanity came rushing back and Rachel remembered what she had forgotten for the moment...he was her enemy, controlling her actions, and denying her the financial freedom she so desperately wanted.

Rachel drew herself up and replied in a cool tone, "Well, of course. I wouldn't want *anyone* to be in danger traveling back to Virginia."

He laughed, thoroughly amused. "What shall I get for you while I'm in Virginia?" he asked, his eyes dancing with merriment.

Rachel thought about that. Perhaps if she had some new silk, Louise could run up a dress for her. Something tantalizing that would turn Sam's head. Cissa taught her that you could always get to a man by being flirtatious. She hated being deceptive. It was not in her nature. And Sam was a man very secure in his manhood and not easily swayed.

Unsure of her own abilities in this area, Rachel feared that her efforts might come across as comical. It galled her that she would think of resorting to such tactics to get her way. But, after all, she reasoned, the money was rightfully hers. She should be able to spend it as she saw fit.

Rachel bit her lip, then, tentatively asked, "Oh—um—would you—uh—bring me some silk?"

His eyebrows rose noticeably. "Silk? I thought...." He shook his head. "Never mind what I thought. What about all your dresses that came down the Ohio?"

"Oh...those? Well..." she said evasively. "I—I just wanted something new."

Rachel squirmed. As expert an attorney as she had heard he was, she was afraid that he would extract from her the reason for such a request. Glancing down at her attire, she desperately needed a fancy dress to attract him. Goodness knows...up until now, he always seemed to catch her at her worst.

She gave a little sigh. But she was having a baby. What on earth made her imagine he would think of her that way in the condition she was in?

"Forget it," she said dismissively and started to turn away.

Sam caught her arm as a teasing smile played across his lips. "Of course, I'll bring you some silk," he nodded, "enough for several new dresses, in fact. Now, what do you think about that?"

Sam's face softened as he reached and caught a strand of her hair. "I'll bring you some ribbon for that black hair and a new hat, as well."

She wrinkled her nose. "I don't wear hats."

He smiled at her skeptical eyes. "This one you will."

Riding from North Star toward town, Sam's senses were stirred. He had felt an attraction to Rachel the first moment he met her, but she was Ransom's wife then. He had stayed strictly away from her and avoided any unnecessary contact with her, treating her with aloofness. He was protecting, first of all, his relationship with God, then, his friendship with Ransom.

Now Ransom was dead. Though he had feelings for her, he wasn't sure if he was ready to progress beyond that. God only knew how difficult she was. And he had too many irons in the fire right now. In addition to his farm, his legal business was growing more quickly than he had anticipated, and, most of all, ministry with Jacob Templeton.

"No. Think I'll just leave things the way they are," he thought. "After all, Ransom hasn't been dead long and Rachel is carrying his child.

Still...she had a wildness about her that excited him.

"Hyah," he yelled as he urged his horse to gallop faster.

CHAPTER EIGHT

IT WAS THE MIDDLE OF DECEMBER. Carefully dressing in one of her prettiest frocks that had been let out in the waist by Louise and wearing her warm cloak, Rachel made another trip to New Wellington. A plan had been hatching in her mind since Sam left for Virginia, and, with all the willpower she had within her, she was going to do her best to bring it to pass.

The day she had met Will on the street, he'd promised that he would help her in whatever way he could. If Sam wouldn't give her the money…her own money, then, perhaps Will would sell her lumber on credit. Not considering how to pay off the debt, she was only concerned with getting what she wanted now.

After countless hours spent fantasizing how she could fulfill her scheme, Rachel decided the best course of action would be to appeal to Will through Ransom's memory. A wistful smile, a little coquetry, and a teary look, if she could manage it, would get her just what she wanted. Rachel was sure of that.

Cissa had taken a lot of time coaching her on how to flirt when she was wooing Ransom. "If only those same tactics worked on

Sam," she thought with a frown. But he was a man, not a boy, and seemed resistant to feminine ploys.

It was unnerving to think that Sam could see right through her. It made her feel defenseless and she disliked the feeling intensely.

The girl in Sam's office seemed to make an impression on him, though, she thought disconsolately, as the scene she had witnessed came rushing back. She felt like an unnoticed sparrow, while Sam was enthralled with an exotic bird like the one that Langdron's store had on display in Virginia.

She stopped by Will's house before making her rounds about town. If anyone knew the gossip in town, it would be Jane. She didn't care much for her snooty sister-in-law, but the blonde had preyed upon her mind.

Though, while on the road to Green River Country, Jane had said, in no uncertain terms, what she thought of Rachel and her free-spirited ways, Rachel was willing to set aside her pride, and worm whatever information she could from her. It was eating at her and she just had to know.

Their house was at the end of town, right on Main Street close by the school.

"Pretty impressive," Rachel thought with envy after she rode up, stepped down, and tied her horse to the hitching rail. It was a large two-story with several men milling around adding the finishing touches. Something along the lines of what Ransom had drawn. She doubted if any politician in the capital city of Philadelphia owned such a magnificent home. Not that she had been to Philadelphia.

She climbed the large, sweeping steps and reaching the massive door, lifted the knocker and struck it.

No one answered.

"Hello," she called.

For a moment Rachel thought she heard a murmur of voices inside.

She knocked again, a little harder this time.

"Hello," she called in her loudest voice. "Hello! Is anybody home?"

"Rachel, dear!" Jane exclaimed, as she opened the door, her body showing the last stages of pregnancy. "So good to see you!" she mewed, sweet as a kitten. "Do come in. I'm sorry for the delay, but you just can't get good help nowadays! Will hired servants for the house, but it takes a while to train them!"

She stepped back and looked Rachel over as she crossed the threshold. "My! How pretty you look today!"

"Thank you, Jane," Rachel responded, feeling better about her visit. It wasn't often that she was on the receiving end of Jane's compliments.

"I had to make a trip into town and wanted to look you up. I'm sorry I missed you the last time I was in New Wellington."

"That's quite all right, Rachel. I've been *so* busy. As you can see, we finally got moved out of that horrid little cabin. Believe me, I didn't let up on Will night or day until he put up this house. Of course, this is only temporary. He's promised to build one of brick."

She sighed with a touch of smugness on her face as she looked around. "The absolute envy of the town, it will be."

Remembering the proprieties she had momentarily forgotten, Jane called, "Nancy!" and a woman appeared in the doorway. Rachel recognized her from their journey to Kentucky and nodded to her. Jane took Rachel's cloak and handed it to Nancy. "Please hang this up."

As Nancy walked away, Jane raised her eyes to the ceiling and whispered, "I told you, it's just so hard to get good help."

Putting her arm around Rachel's waist, Jane led her to the parlor. Will's carpentry business in Virginia had provided the family with fine furniture. Glancing into the dining room on the other side of the hall she saw the familiar massive, mahogany table with enough chairs to accommodate all of the Templeton family.

The sideboard and buffet, which displayed gilded girandoles, presented to Jane on her wedding day by her mother, appropriately reflected the charm of the house Will had built. In the parlor were the familiar pieces that Will and his brothers had created, in addition to imported furniture. In the corner was a French chamber harp inlaid with mother of pearl. A pair of French oak cabinets with ebony veneer, pewter inlay, gilt bronze mounts, and inset Japanese lacquer panels with black marble tops complemented the beauty of the harp.

The Templeton family had exquisite taste in furnishings. The fact that Ransom had dreamed about creating his own home of similar affluence was a reflection of what he had grown up with and she was determined, if it took the last breath of her body, to make his dreams come true.

The windows were devoid of drapery. "Soon to be rectified," Jane said. The material was on its way down the Ohio. Will had gone to a great deal of trouble to get all of their provisions here.

As Jane led Rachel to the rosewood sofas with their lush cushioning, she began to whine. "After all, he made me leave Wellington and my family. I miss Mother and Father dreadfully and am afraid I'll never see them again," she said tearfully.

"Can you imagine? Not even post service here. Someone has to make a trip to Cobb's Corner twice a month for the post. How barbaric this place is! And look at *me* having our second baby."

She gasped and put her hand over her mouth. Dropping her fingertips to her chin, she exclaimed, "Oh, my dear, I've heard you're pregnant with Ransom's baby."

Clasping Rachel's hands, Jane declared, "How simply awful for you!"

Rachel squirmed and her face looked like she had just swallowed the bad-tasting tonic that Doctor Stone was fond of handing out in the spring. She didn't like the way Jane was talking.

"I don't think it's so awful," Rachel said as she drew her brows together and pulled against Jane's clasp. "I'm looking forward to having this baby," she said defensively. "It's a part of Ransom that will live on."

"How romantic you make it all sound," Jane said loftily, leaning back into the plush upholstery. "But raising a child on your own won't be easy," she advised. "It's hard enough when you're married. Of course with Will, it's nearly impossible," Jane said sourly. "He's always so busy with all his business ventures. No time for me or Little Jake. Sometimes I think it might have been better if I had never married him. But, he was so charming," she sighed. "Charming, that is, until after we married. Now what I want or think carries no weight with him at all."

"Jane!" cried Rachel aghast. "Surely, you don't really feel that way."

"Oh, don't I?" she spoke through gritted teeth, steely bitterness in her face. "Believe me, if I had it to do over, I would *never* have married Will Templeton. There were several others who wanted my hand, you know," she said with a saucy toss of her head. "But he was so sure of himself and what he wanted." She dabbed at her eyes with her hankie and glanced down at her swollen belly. "And just look at me now...pregnant and miserable."

Anxious to change the subject, Rachel blurted out what had been on her mind since her meeting at Sam's office.

"Jane," she said, "I ran into a girl in town that I've never seen before. Tall, blonde, you know—you know the kind—beautiful."

Jane brightened. "Oh, that would have to be Doctor Stone's granddaughter. You remember, don't you? He has two sons that settled this valley before we came. Their names are Claude and Lucien. That's why they call it Stone Valley. Well—let me tell you—Claude has two sons and a daughter. Her name is Claudia. I hear she is absolutely thrilled that New Wellington has been established so that now she can have friends and beaux."

Jane leaned forward and lowering her voice, whispered, "And confidentially, I also heard that she is after Sam. They've been in each other's company on more than one occasion. After all, he is the most eligible bachelor in town, as a property owner, attorney, *and* minister. And, of course, wouldn't you know it? Elizabeth set up a little get-together for them at the parsonage," she said, all-knowingly. "It could be," she mused as she placed a finger against her cheek, "that we will be hearing matrimonial news soon."

If Jane's story was true, then it was indeed Claudia she had seen in Sam's office. She'd felt an unfamiliar pang since that day and now faced the reason why. How could she compete with such a lovely girl? If she hadn't been able to worm her will out of Sam before, how could she expect to now that she was pregnant and unsightly? And if he didn't return until after the baby was born, well...he would look upon her in a maternal way.

As though the air in the room suddenly stifled her, Rachel wanted desperately to get out of there. She smoothed her dress and started to rise.

Seeing Rachel's sudden flurry, Jane, immediately on the alert, asked, "Is there another reason you are in town today, Rachel? Pardon me, if I may be so blunt."

"I…uh…" smiling sweetly, Rachel answered, "just wanted to see everyone again and I have some business to discuss with Will."

"Oh?" Jane asked. "Such as?"

The old biddy, Rachel thought and then laughed. Jane certainly wasn't old but that was the best she could come up with. She said as offhandedly as she could manage: "I just need to put in an order of lumber."

"Lumber?"

"Yes, lumber," Rachel said, nodding.

"But, Rachel, whatever for?" Jane asked as she searched Rachel's face curiously. "Surely you're not building some business in town, are you?"

"No. No. Nothing such as that," Rachel answered. "I've decided to build a home on my property."

"Oh, of course," Jane remarked, remembering where Rachel was living. "I know what it's like to live in a cabin." An unpleasant look came into Jane's eyes.

She said cruelly, "But you're used to that, aren't you? I mean, being raised in one in Virginia."

Rachel should have expected that remark. It hadn't taken Jane long to revert back to her former behavior. Especially, since Jane felt Rachel was far from being quality folk. Jane had tormented her from time to time in Virginia and on the road here to Kentucky, but Rachel had tried to deal with it the best she could.

Looking at Jane, Rachel wondered, *Why did I ever think that Jane might have mended ways?* Although, she had to concede, Jane did make an effort at times. But still, Jane had a mean streak and it was often directed at her.

"You know that I was, Jane. It's just that Ransom planned on building a fine home on our land and I want to carry out his wishes. I've decided now is the time to do it."

"Well...yes...I can see why you would want to build a house," Jane remarked slowly, more to herself than to Rachel.

"Good," Rachel responded, glad that it was settled.

After a few seconds of thoughtful silence, Jane spoke up again. "But isn't that Sam Spencer's decision to make?" Jane asked. "I heard that he's executor over your finances," she added with a smirk.

A flush rose in Rachel's cheeks. What business was it of hers? She struggled to stay calm and appear unaffected by Jane's remarks.

"Yes, normally...but Sam had to go back East. I talked to him about it before he left. It will be just fine. Really, it will." She bit her lip on that.

The corners of Jane's lips curved into a small smile. "You know, Rachel, I never really did understand why Ransom made his will the way he did, with Sam as the executor. After all, you don't really know Sam very well. Truthfully, I've often wondered, why not Will or Jacob or even James? But...who knows? Maybe it was all for the best."

Jane patted Rachel's hand in a conciliatory manner and said, "I think sometimes men regard us as just silly little things, incapable of making a sensible decision on our own." Resentment seeped back into Jane's face. "I know for certain that Will feels that way."

Rachel did rise then and started for the door. "I really must go, Jane. So much to do, you know. Come and visit North Star sometime."

Jane rose also, followed her, and frowned. "I doubt that you'll catch me out there, Rachel. I'm just not into the country life." Glancing around, her lofty attitude returned. "After all, you can see what we have here."

Jane's face suddenly brightened as she remembered her position as hostess. "But do stop in whenever you're in New Wellington."

After retrieving her cloak, Rachel was glad to get out of there. She had a sudden urge to take a bath. If she could wash Jane's attitude off her, she would. She had tolerated Jane, though at times she acted whiney. Now with her smug and condescending ways, she was almost impossible to be around.

CHAPTER NINE

THE LUMBER MILL WAS IN FULL OPERATION when Rachel arrived.

Wagons lined the entrance awaiting the lumber to be loaded onto them. She had spent a lot of time in the mill in Wellington where Ransom had taught her some carpentry skills and she found herself relaxing in the atmosphere. She was tense when she arrived, but the mill's activity calmed her.

She loved the smell of fresh-cut lumber and wished she could spend time here. "But, as in Wellington," she thought with a sigh, "it would not be seen as appropriate here, either."

Rachel spotted Will overseeing operations, a haggard look on his face. She had never seen him look so tired. Most of the men looked familiar except for a couple whom she thought must be the sons of Doctor Stone.

Seeing Rachel picking her way through stacks of lumber as she walked toward him, Will turned and quickly crossed to her, a smile widening his mouth.

"Rachel!" he exclaimed as he took her hand.

After he had settled her in his makeshift office where he sat on the edge of the desk exchanging chitchat, she changed the thread of the conversation.

"Will...remember when you said that if there was anything I needed...to just ask?" Rachel cooed, batting her eyes as she looked up at him. Cissa had taught her that.

"Sure, Rachel, anything for my sister-in-law, you know that. What can I do for you today?"

She began to think this might turn out to be easier than she had anticipated. The fact that she was carrying his dead brother's baby assured her of almost anything. Rachel let her cloak drop away from her dress, making sure his attention was drawn to the slight mound of her belly.

"Well—you know Ransom's dream was to build a fine home on our land."

Will nodded.

Rachel drew Ransom's drawing from her reticule. She unfolded the parchment and presented it to him.

Will held the sketch in his hands and studied it thoughtfully. She couldn't read the expression on his face and soon she asked, "You like it, don't you?"

"Like it?" He looked up suddenly and smiled warmly. "Like it? I love it! Ransom had talent, that's for sure," Will folded the plans and handed them back to her. "I'd hold on to this for a keepsake of him."

She bit her lip. Will didn't understand. He thought she was being nostalgic and sharing some memento of Ransom.

"No, Will," she said. "That's not why I'm here."

"What then?" he asked, puzzled.

"I want to build that house. Ransom's house."

Will got up. He'd told her he would do anything for her, but if she was expecting him to throw everything aside and build that house for her, he just didn't have the time.

"Rachel, I'm so busy now that I can't possibly spend time at North Star to build your house."

"You misunderstood me, Will. I'm building it myself."

"You?" he asked, surprised.

"Oh, Will!" she agonized, "I'd do just about anything to make his dream come true. Do you think you could make a deal on some lumber with me?"

He frowned at her, hooking his thumbs in his trousers. "This is a pretty big job to undertake, Rachel. I'm not sure you can manage it."

"Well, I have Frank and he's ever so smart and handy." Since that little bit of information did nothing to wipe the doubtful look from Will's face, she added, "And Sam's bringing help back from Virginia."

"Speaking of Sam," Will said, "what's he got to say about this? He never mentioned building a home to me before he left."

Oh, great! Rachel thought as her brow knitted slightly. She should never have mentioned Sam for she never counted on him being brought into the conversation. Well, by hook or crook, she would get what she came for.

"Oh, Sam and I talked about it," she said with an airy gesture, refusing to meet his gaze. "He knows how set I am on raising Ransom's baby in a fine home instead of that little cabin I'm living in. You know Ransom would only want the best for his child."

She looked up and with a bright smile, asked, "Don't you, Will?" For added emphasis, she leaned forward and placed her hand on his forearm, her eyes willing him to say "yes".

His brows drew together in thought. Rachel was right. No sense in having Ransom's child living in a cabin with a dirt floor. After all, she had married a Templeton and was carrying a Templeton baby.

Encasing her small hand in his, he finally uttered, "All right, Rachel, as long as you've got Sam's approval."

Releasing her hand, he said, "I won't make a deal."

Her heart sank at hearing those words but soared at the next ones.

"But I'll tell you what I will do. I'll *give* the lumber to you. No charge."

Rachel was ecstatic, but refrained from throwing her arms around Will's neck. No wonder all the men liked Will. Generous to a fault he was.

"Oh, Will!" she sparkled. "I'll be forever grateful to you!"

Touching his arm again, she told him: "And if Ransom was alive, you know he would be, too!"

With a wave of his hand, Will commented, "Yes, I know."

Glancing at the workmen, his mind already moving on to the task at hand, he told her, "But you can see how busy I am right now. The mill is going night and day and I just don't have the time right now."

As she rose from her chair, he placed an arm around her shoulders and walked her out of the office. "But listen, Rachel. I'll have some of it ready in about a week. Just have Frank come around and pick up the order."

She left the mill feeling triumphant. Sam hadn't won. She'd had her way. It was a heady feeling to know that she had managed to maneuver around Sam.

For once, Rachel felt that he did not control every aspect of her life.

"And who knows?" she thought, her mind whirling, "Maybe I could finagle some furniture for my house from Will. It doesn't hurt that I'm pregnant. Works in my favor, in fact. Won't Sam be surprised to see what I've done!"

A little worry did cross her mind as to what would happen when Sam found out. He was definitely not someone to cross. But she would think about that later. She wasn't going to let anything dim her glow of victory. And what could he do to her, anyway?

"After all," she reasoned, "I don't belong to Sam."

CHAPTER TEN

JANUARY PASSED INTO FEBRUARY. The hard freezes of February transitioned into the blustery weather of March. Before spring arrived, Rachel went into labor. Her child was a son, with downy, auburn hair and nearly an exact image of Ransom. She named him Payne, Ransom's middle name.

When April appeared with soft, southerly winds ushering in warm weather, Sam still had not returned. Rachel feared that something had happened to him and as much as told her father so.

She had asked Sam not to travel the Ohio. And though she and Sam had their moments, the worry that some mishap had occurred, gnawed at her constantly.

The baby was a month old and becoming tired of lying-in, Rachel stepped outside the cabin and sat down on the log trestle John had made for sitting.

The wild plums were blooming, splays of white in the greening forest. A bit of sun beamed where she sat, beckoning Rachel to raise her face, close her eyes, and smile at the warming shaft that stole its way through the trees displaying the first tender, lime-green leaves of spring.

As she sat lost in the feeling that everything was right with the world, she heard the sound of hooves and the whinny of a horse coming across the field. Peering through the trees, she saw Sam riding toward the cabin and with him were strangers. Three men, one older and two younger, were following Sam's lead. A woman in her early twenties, obviously with child, was last in line.

Her curiosity waned momentarily as she caught sight of Sam's red hair. Her heart beat a bit faster and she realized in that instant just how much she had missed him.

"Strange that I should feel this way," she thought, casting her face down, hiding a smile.

Before Sam reached the cabin, a feeling of guilty panic struck her at the sight of his face. She started to turn as though to run away and realized she had nowhere to run. When Sam found out that she had finagled her way into getting lumber from Will, he would be furious. And though he'd held his temper in check with her in the past, a warning flashed through her mind that perhaps she had gone too far this time.

He drew up at the cabin and swung lightly to the ground. As he removed his hat and placed it on the saddle, Rachel nervously searched his face trying to determine what mood he was in.

As he walked toward her, she called a greeting to him, beckoning her prettiest smile. Thank goodness she was dressed in one of her better frocks! Her hair freshly washed and cascading around her face made her feel pretty. As his eyes went swiftly over her, she knew he thought her pretty, too.

"I heard in town you'd had the baby," he commented. Leaning down, he pushed the blanket away from Payne's small face. After a few moments, he remarked, "Ransom all over again, I'd say." He grew silent.

Frowning, he stated, "I was told you refused to stay with Jacob. Pulling the blanket back over the baby, he asked, "No trouble with the birth?"

"No, not really. He was just a little early, that's all." She smiled up at him brightly. "Thanks for asking."

He searched her face as she asked, "How are you, Sam? You've been away a long time, longer than I expected."

His blue eyes grew suddenly alert, and he caught her gaze and held it until a blush crept into her cheeks.

"Miss me?" Sam finally asked.

"I—I...." she stammered and her blush was complete. Glancing toward the others standing patiently by, she asked, "Who are they?"

Sam motioned for them to draw nearer. "These are your indentures, Rachel." The older man in his forties was introduced as Caleb Burton and his sons, Luke and Mark. The woman, in her early twenties and large with child, was Mary McKinnon.

After turning them over to Frank and Louise, Sam took the baby from Rachel, handed Payne to Louise, and with a determined look steered Rachel outside again.

He motioned toward the creek and said, "Come with me."

Not a question or suggestion, but an order.

It was on the tip of her tongue to resist and she nearly pulled back. "But I can't leave the baby," she lamented.

He tightened his hold and said, "The baby will be fine for a few minutes."

"Oh, dear!" she thought. "Now he's going to talk about the lumber I got from Will."

Rachel turned back and mutely asked for help from Louise. Louise's only response was a slight lifting of her shoulders.

As they walked in silence, her mind flitted about, trying to think of a way to delay the inevitable. Reaching the creek, she blurted out, "How was your trip, Sam? Did you have any trouble? You were gone so long."

He plucked off a twig and leaned back against a tree, drawing up his knee, and propping his foot against it.

"It wasn't the best time of year to travel. The Ohio was frozen, but, all in all, at least I've got the warm weather ahead of me to make some inroads on my property."

His eyes flickered over her. "You seem to have lost some weight. Been back at it full steam since the baby came? No? I expect you will be soon. Now that your indentures have arrived, some of the load will be taken off you. Although, I daresay, you'll probably work as hard as they."

"Well, what if I do..." she began to ruffle.

He threw the twig down. "Really, Rachel," he raised his voice, suddenly angry. "You've got the baby now. It's time to take it easy."

"What do you expect me to do? Lie around all day?" she cried hotly.

"What I expect and what you actually do, are two different things," he cynically countered. "You never take my advice."

She nearly retorted, "I never asked for it," but choked back the words. He was annoyed. She knew it and with great restraint changed the subject.

"By the way, Sam, why did you buy a pregnant woman?" she asked coolly. "I don't need another woman around here. I've got Louise."

His eyebrows rose. "I have the distinct impression that you're not the domestic type and could use some extra help in that area," he told her bluntly.

She was miffed, but couldn't deny what he said was true.

"Besides," he continued, softening his tone, "she was treated pretty badly and I felt she deserved a break."

Eyes opening wide, "What happened to her?" she asked.

He drew a deep breath. "She was working off her indenture to a married couple. The man forced her and she became with child. The court blamed her and not the man and added two more years to her indenture."

"But, that's ridiculous!" Rachel cried. "How could the court rule that way?"

He shrugged. "That's the way it is, Rachel. They often rule against the indentured."

Her forehead wrinkled in sympathy as she pondered that for a moment. "But what about the baby?" she asked.

Sam pushed himself away from the tree. "That's the irony of it, Rachel. The baby will be your indenture until it's twenty-one. That's the law of the land."

"Well," she cast her eyes down, forehead drawing a slight frown and pondered aloud, "I'll just set it free."

"You can't do that, Rachel. There are laws and Mary is contracted unto you. And I should also let you know, there's a thing called 'Freedom Dues'."

"Freedom dues?"

"Yes. When their contract is fulfilled you must give them a few acres of land, a year's worth of corn, arms, a cow, and new clothes. Think it over. It's to your advantage, really."

Her eyes shot up to his face. "But the mother is free in what— two more years? What about the baby, then?"

"You can let the mother stay on and manage some small salary for her. However, the child is to remain here until the age of twenty-one. That's not my decision, but the order of lawmakers."

Incredible! That the child would stay here until then. Sounds a little like slavery.

Putting all that aside, her mind began to click, making a checklist of things to do. Put up more cabins immediately, men's and women's quarters. *Oh, why hadn't I done that already! I knew Sam was bringing servants.* Though an extra room had been added to her cabin, a cabin had never been raised for Frank and Louise and they were cramped in the small space with her. That needed to be rectified. She also hadn't expected Sam to bring home another woman.

"Where will Mary sleep until her quarters are built, especially with a baby coming?" she thought. "I suppose she could stay in my little bedroom with me for the time being. Thank goodness for the extra help now! I need a bigger barn and with their assistance I could also build that home with the lumber stored in that addition that Frank built to the barn."

At that thought, her eyes darted to Sam and found he was watching her with an expression she couldn't fathom. But something told her that he knew what she had done. Was that something merely her guilty conscience? Maybe if she put his mind on something else....

"Sam," said Rachel, "I've been thinking that I need to add to my livestock. You know this would be the perfect time with all this extra help."

"I've thought of that already. Will and I are going to Logan County to purchase some hogs. You can get the servants to prepare for them while we're gone, or if you like I'll talk to Frank about it. You can either let the hogs forage in the woods or build pens for about...say...fifty."

"Oh? You talked to—?" Rachel began, and then she saw the look in his eyes and stopped.

"I did," he pointedly said. "Which brings me to the reason why I asked you out here."

You didn't exactly ask me.

Rachel's heart began to beat faster, and she made a quarter turn as though to escape.

He spoke lightly but there was anger in his eyes. "Did you honestly think I wouldn't find out about your little—or—should I say—large—extraction from Will? What excuse did you use to convince him to give you the lumber...your pregnancy?"

She squirmed, and her eyes fell.

"I thought so. Of course, I already knew. I saw Will in town yesterday and he told me. You took advantage of him, Rachel, knowing that Ransom's baby was a soft spot with him. You've always been straightforward and I've always admired and respected you for that, even if we do disagree at times. I'm disappointed in you, Rachel. I never thought you would stoop to feminine tactics just to get your way."

Resentment welled in her at the implication of his words and her jaw line tightened.

"I'm only trying to do what Ransom wanted," she stated with injured dignity. "Those were *his* plans, not mine. He's dead, and I have his child, and I'll carry out his wishes no matter what anyone says or thinks."

Sam looked into her tense face, his own expression inscrutable. Something flickered behind his eyes, but he said nothing.

"You can condemn me if you want, Sam," she continued, "but I refuse to let anyone stop me or get in the way. I'm keeping the lumber and I *will* build that house! Ransom's house!"

He searched her eyes. "So be it, Rachel," he quietly informed her. "I'm going to try to square it with Will, if possible. My instincts tell me he won't take payment now. But you owe it to him and should try to find a way to pay him for the lumber that he gave you."

"Me?" she asked in an astonished voice, putting her hand on her chest. "How can I do that? *You* have control of my money. If he won't take the money from you, I don't know what *I* can do about it."

He shrugged and looked away. "That's *your* problem."

He didn't raise his voice with those last words, but they cracked like a whip. Had he exploded...and Rachel wished he had...she could argue back.

Her mind was spinning. What on earth could she ever do to earn enough money to pay Will? She had no skills to speak of. Certainly not sewing and her cooking would never earn any good report.

And now, after secretly gloating that she had obtained the lumber after he had refused her permission, she felt that she had lost something. Something she could not quite define, but wanted desperately to win back.

What was it that he had said—respect and admiration? Yes, that was it. She hadn't known he held her in high regard, for they argued so...rather *she* argued.

Sam was disappointed. She could endure his over-solicitous ways, the fact that he held the upper hand and would do so until she turned twenty-five, but she could not bear his disappointment.

Her eyes sought his face, desperately hoping she was wrong. His remote eyes came back to her and something in them made her shiver. She knew she had lost him. That word "lost" clanged frighteningly in her mind.

"Lost him? But he's never belonged to me," she reasoned. "I never really possessed him, yet—yet somehow I know he's left me. Oh! I'm so confused! If I could only turn back time, I would do things differently."

From the pit of her stomach, something was reaching up and its tentacles were squeezing her heart.

Suddenly, she felt like crying.

Sam turned as though the subject was closed and walked toward the cabin, leaving her feeling abandoned.

Everything within her wanted to run after him and beg his forgiveness. Surely, she could make him understand! She had to!

Her hand clutched the skirt of her dress as she took a step toward his retreating back and then stopped. He didn't want her—didn't want anything to do with her—not now.

Taking his hat from the saddle, he settled it on his head, stepped up on his horse, and rode away without so much as a backward glance.

She had won—yet, she had lost. She'd gotten her way, but it was not making her happy. She knew Sam detested phoniness and manipulation.

Goodness knows, according to him, he had seen enough of that already with the women he had known.

It all seemed such a terrible mess now. If only she had control of her own money, if she hadn't cajoled Will into giving her the lumber, if she had only waited—if, if, if!

She turned her head because it hurt too much to watch Sam ride away. Sighing, she realized she would miss him making such ado about her needs and fussing at her.

Hearing the sound of hooves dying away, feeling miserable and dejected, she leaned her head on the side of the tree still warm from Sam's body...and wept.

Sam was hurt—deeply hurt. In addition to her wild beauty and stubbornness, he had been attracted by her innocence...innocence that had remained untouched in spite of divorce, death, and a sundry other things. The hypocrisy of society had been as foreign to her as to a newborn.

Free-spirited as a bird soaring in all its glory, Rachel had been. He had thought her different, not like the many other women he had consorted with in the past.

No other woman had been able to touch him like she had. Now, she was learning the scheming tactics of the devious and this wounded him deeply. He supposed every man sought a place...a special place...a sanctuary really, with someone of her integrity.

As no other woman had ever done, she had been slowly chipping away the tough shell around his heart until it was difficult to think of anything else but her.

In those long days of waiting to get home, he had anxiously willed the Ohio to thaw so that he might return to her. He longed to see her with an intensity he had never known. She attracted him more than any woman, and now he felt a need to protect himself from any further disillusionment.

He would have to draw away from her again for his own heart's sake.

CHAPTER ELEVEN

MARY MCKINNON HAD HER BABY. It was a tiny girl whose head was covered with wads of curly, blonde hair. After much discussion in the household, the child was called Margaret, nicknamed "Maggie."

Jane and Will had a girl, Elizabeth, whom they called "Beth," and James and Cissa had a girl named Anne.

Rachel was attending Sunday service every week now that her help had arrived. The Templeton family took Payne over completely on Sundays, persuading Rachel to spend the day with them.

Sam was always at church but never ventured more than a perfunctory nod—aloof and remote, impersonal courtesy.

Of course, as Sam expected, Will had turned down Sam's offer to pay for the lumber. Sam had intended to pay for the lumber out of his own funds and that fact was revealed on Sunday when Rachel approached Will.

She had spent many a night trying to figure a way to repay him and finally came up with a solution.

Requesting a walk out-of-doors with him after dinner, she informed him, "Will, I just feel so frightful about the lumber you gave me for the new house and I feel I should repay you in some way. I—I think I've found a way to do it."

Will waved his hand in the air. "That's not necessary, Rachel. I can well afford it. As a matter-of-fact, Sam offered to pay for the lumber himself, but, of course, I wouldn't hear of it."

"Sam?" she asked in surprise. "Sam offered to pay for the lumber—out of his own money?"

"Sure," he said, as he picked his teeth with a sharp sliver of wood, an act, in public, that Elizabeth would heartily disapprove of. "But I wouldn't accept it. Money's not that important to me."

Rachel was reeling from shock. She knew Sam was very well off financially, but why should he, of all people, want to pay for her lumber? She was nothing to him. At least, she didn't think she was.

"Will...you know that I don't have control of my money," she said, glancing down at her hands and coloring slightly.

"Of course," he agreed, "That's how Ransom wanted it."

She overlooked his remark and said, "Will, I'd still like to pay for the lumber. Please let me," she pleaded.

"Now, just how could you pay, Rachel?"

"Well...I've been thinking and I've come up with—."

"Rachel," Will interrupted, "believe me, it's really not important."

"To me it is," she insisted. "Call it pride, if you like."

Touching him lightly on the arm, she said, "Listen, Will, I've thought of a solution. Though I can't pay you the money, I would like to work off the debt at Templeton Store."

"Rachel, forget about it. You don't have to come and work for me," he adamantly replied.

Hating to evoke Ransom's memory again, she ventured, "But, Will, I think Ransom would be pleased if I did."

Will stopped walking and looked down at her, puzzled. "Why? What does Ransom have to do with this?"

She looked up at him and in that moment realized Sam had never mentioned her little deception. What a strange man Sam was. Most other men would have spread it all over town in no time flat.

Rachel dropped her eyes. "Ransom would never have taken advantage of anyone," she admitted as she withdrew her hand.

He was silent for a moment. He placed a finger under her cheek, forcing her to look up. "Is that what you did, Rachel?" he asked softly. "You took advantage of me?"

Will may very well end up hating me if I admit to the truth. I used deceit and now I need to make it right, even if it means falling out of Will's good graces.

She looked away as he released his finger from her chin. "I might as well come clean, Will," she spoke with frankness, "I did. Sam would not allow me to buy the lumber before he left for Virginia, so I resorted to using Ransom's memory to get what I wanted."

Will was quiet as he searched her face. It had cost her to tell the truth, Will saw that. He was glad she had a strong conscience. It was of little consequence to him if she had messed up. What was important, she was willing to make it right. Throwing his pick away, he smiled an easy smile.

"It doesn't matter to me, Rachel, but if it's that important to you…then start sometime next week. A few months should do it."

Rachel looked up at him. In that moment, though she didn't quite understand it, a bond had formed between them that had never been there before. He thought of her not as a sister-in-law that he had previously considered somewhat immature, but now as an equal.

She knew in those few self-revealing moments she had gained a respect that had not been afforded her in the past.

She left for North Star that day feeling more mature and self-confident than she had in a very long time.

Sam was surprised to learn that Rachel was working off her debt at Templeton Store. He had avoided her for weeks and, other than whatever information Frank supplied him with, knew nothing about her affairs. She had altered her appearance, much to his dismay, and her hairstyle was changed to the fashion of the day. Preferring her hair worn down to reflect her free-spirited personality, he was disappointed, though he readily admitted the new style only enhanced her beauty, and the bolts of cloth he had purchased in Virginia had been made into several new dresses displaying her maturity.

In spite of it all, he often found himself hoping for a sight of her as he walked through New Wellington. When he caught glimpses of her from time to time, he always retreated in the opposite direction, yet all the while watching her from a distance. He never frequented Templeton Store, except when he knew she wasn't there.

Meeting Tom for lunch at New Wellington House one day, he paused inside the entrance when he saw her sitting alone at a table. Debating whether to cross the room and speak to her, he was hit suddenly in the back with the door.

"Wha—?" Tom asked as he pressed through the door. Sam recovered and turned to face him.

"Sorry," Sam sheepishly offered. "It's my fault. I should have moved on in."

"Sure," Tom said, sweeping off his hat. "Let's get a table. I'm starved. Hey!" he pointed, "there's Rachel. Come on...let's eat with her."

As Tom walked toward Rachel with Sam following, Rachel looked up eagerly at him, a smile on her face.

"Rachel! You don't mind if a couple of hungry men sit at your table, do you?"

She laughed. "Tom! No, of course not," sweeping her hand to a chair. Sam stepped out from behind Tom and Rachel froze as the smile slipped slowly away. "No, of course not," she repeated, warily observing Sam.

Lunch was strained, to say the least. Sam was guarded and barely offered anything beyond a monosyllable, often shaking his head in silent acquiescence to Tom's ramblings. Yet, Sam's eyes frequently sought her own as he sat across the small table from her. Serious eyes—laughter gone—with a hint of hunger in them that seemed to say, "I miss you."

As naïve as Rachel was...still, she recognized the message in those blue eyes.

She missed him too.

CHAPTER TWELVE

"I DON'T KNOW, JANE," RACHEL HESITATED. "I'm not that fond of parties."

That was true. She would rather attend a large social function where she could melt into the background than small affairs where the agonizing task of making conversation often had her fumbling and tongue-tied.

"That may be. But, Rachel, you are a Templeton, and, therefore, are expected to attend a Templeton party," Jane stated emphatically.

I was a Winslow first.

"And Sam," Jane continued, "would be terribly offended if you did not attend to receive his father and cousin from Virginia."

Rachel doubted that. Though there was a cordial peace between them now, Sam had not sought her out, and he stayed well away from North Star. She found herself hoping Sam might walk through the door at the store. But he never did.

Rachel sighed. Sam probably wouldn't notice if she was at the party at all. And she didn't particularly care to meet Sam's father and this cousin of his. If the cousin was anything like Sam, she was sure they would not get on.

Since that strained lunch at New Wellington House with Sam and Tom, there had been little conversation between her and Sam. He never sought her out and acted as though she didn't exist, though his eyes said differently. Even at church, his eyes followed her. But they were so serious.

Their relationship was at an impasse and she was frustrated. No longer going to his office for funds, she sent Frank, instead, with her requests. She couldn't appear to be running after Sam.

Jane chided, "It's important to make a good impression as Sam's father is a congressman and his cousin, an aide. Who knows? Perhaps a Templeton will be appointed to the Kentucky Congress. I overheard Jacob talking about the possibility. Imagine me," Jane clasped her hands to her chest and closed her eyes, "a congressman's wife."

Rachel rolled her eyes. Jane was the moodiest person she had ever met. One day she was talking about leaving Will, and the next, ensconced in politics.

Sizing Rachel from head to toe, "And by the way, do you have anything suitable for a party?" Jane asked. "Surely you can't wear your day-dress."

Rachel dropped her head. "I'll talk to Elizabeth about it," she mumbled as she toyed with the folds of her dress. It was a pretty frock, but in Jane's eyes, nothing of hers was ever quite good enough.

Rachel had just finished dressing for the party when wheels sounded outside the cabin.

Practically tripping over the hem of her dress, she hastened out of her room.

Louise was cleaning up the supper dishes. "It's Sam," she commented, jerking her head in that direction.

"Sam?" Rachel asked wide-eyed, as she flew to the small window.

Louise nodded.

"What's he doing here?" Rachel whispered, drawing back into hiding.

"I don't know, but you'd better answer the door," Louise said as the second knock sounded a little louder.

Rachel hesitated, then finally moved to the door, lifted the latch and opened it halfway.

"Hello, Sam," Rachel said.

"Good evening, Rachel," he nodded, giving her an appreciative look.

"I thought you were supposed to be at the party."

"Well...obviously I'm not...yet," he said.

"Yes...um...I see."

"Aren't you going to ask me in?" he chided.

Rachel didn't and instead stood dumfounded. "What on earth are you doing here?" she finally asked.

Sam locked his fingers together in front of him. "That's gracious of you," he said dryly. "I came by to escort you to the party."

When she didn't answer, he commented, "Well, it appears that you're ready to go."

"With you?" she questioned.

"Of course, with me...who else?"

"But you never asked me to go with you."

"I didn't think I had to. You can't go traipsing off into the night by yourself and since my property adjoins yours, this seemed the best solution."

Her ire began to rise. Sam had avoided her for the last few weeks and now he shows up at her door and just assumes she will go with him?

"Well, that might be *your* solution, Sam, but I planned on driving my wagon."

Sam grinned as he made an airy gesture toward his buggy. "Oh, but, dear lady, how could you turn down such a fine chariot as this? And all the trouble I went through to get it, no less."

He took her off guard. In fact, he was downright charming and refused to be baited into a fight.

Glancing at the buggy, "Where did you get it?" she asked suspiciously.

"Rented it from Cromwell's," he volunteered. "So—," giving a bow, "fair maiden—how about it?" Sam implored and then shifted his stance. "Want to ride with me or chance running into some ferocious animal in the dark?"

"I could run into a ferocious animal whether I'm with you or not," Rachel said, her lips curling down into a frown.

"True. True," he agreed. "But there's safety in numbers and I don't think you have room for a rifle in that fancy frock."

"So he *did* notice what I'm wearing," she thought smugly, silently thanking Elizabeth for her dressmaking skills. The dress she was wearing was 'the style of the day' Elizabeth had informed her. Like the dress in the dressmaker's shop, it was the rage of European fashion.

"All right," she relented after hesitating a few moments. She supposed it *would* be safer to have someone to ride home with in the dark. "Just let me say goodbye to the baby."

"So...where are your father and cousin?" Rachel asked as the horse trotted toward town.

"They're staying at the inn."

"And you're not staying there with them?"

He was silent for a brief moment. "I was."

She turned to look at him. "Was?"

"Yes."

"Then why—?"

Cutting her off, "There were a few things to take care of at my place," he hastily said.

Turning back to look straight ahead, Rachel was utterly confused. He had stayed away from her and now....

As they drew up in front of Will and Jane's home, the draped windows were aglow with crystal chandeliers bearing dozens of candles, and shadows of guests moving about were cast from their brilliant light. Rachel's heart began to beat faster at the sound of music. She didn't like parties and swallowed hard, anticipating a torturous evening at New Wellington's first formal social event.

Sam alighted from the buggy, tethered the horse, and crossed to her side. Extending his hand toward her, he was taken aback by the panicked look on her face.

"Rachel?" his brows drew together. "Is there something wrong?"

"I—I," she stammered as the strains of music filled her ears. She was suddenly shy. She would be expected to dance, of course. And dancing did not come easily to her. Nor did making conversation.

His face softened as he recognized her predicament. "It's only a party, Rachel, and you know most of the people here."

"I...." she moaned.

"I'll stay with you," he promised. "It will be fine, you'll see. Come on," he coaxed.

Rachel looked down at him. He didn't really understand. It was easy for him. Sam was used to a lifestyle with fancy parties, while she had lived secluded in the country.

"Besides," he smiled, "I want you to meet my father."

His fingers touched her fingertips.

It's not fair for me to keep him from the party. But then again, if I had driven myself, neither he nor I would be in this situation. I probably would have gone back home.

"Come," he urged.

Cautiously, she took the hand offered to her, and closing his fingers over her own, he helped her from the buggy. He refused to release her hand, and as he walked into the massive entry hall at her side, his father and cousin stood in the receiving line greeting the guests.

Glancing their way, Sam's cousin gazed at Rachel as she approached.

"What is that you're saying?" his cousin said, turning back to Jane. "Oh, yes, Doctor and Mrs. Stone. Delighted you could come," he smiled, displaying even white teeth. Kissing Mrs. Stone's hand, his eyes strayed again to Rachel. Straightening his back, he nodded and smiled once more at the doctor.

"Rachel," Sam announced, "I'd like to introduce you to my father, Oliver Spencer. Father, Rachel Templeton."

"Mr. Spencer," she murmured and curtsied.

He smiled and it was Sam's smile in an older face. His red hair, though streaked with shafts of silver, was reminiscent of Sam's, and he had the same striking cornflower-blue eyes.

"Rachel, I'm so pleased we finally meet. I've heard a great deal about you," Oliver informed her.

"About me?" she asked, astonished.

"Yes, Sam's told me—."

"Excuse me, Father. Rachel," Sam interrupted, "this is my cousin, Hayden Spencer. Hayden, I'd like to present Rachel

Templeton. *Mrs.* Templeton, that is," casting Hayden a warning look.

Hayden cocked an eyebrow at Sam as he took Rachel's hand. No resemblance to Sam that she could see. Hayden, somber with his sandy hair and green eyes, belied the playful nature he possessed.

"*Mrs.* Templeton, it's truly my pleasure," Hayden smiled and bent to kiss her hand.

She fluttered. No one had ever been so bold as to kiss her hand. Not even Ransom.

"You've kept this beautiful creature under wraps, Sam?" Hayden taunted him.

Sam pressed his lips firmly together.

"You must save a dance for me, dear lady," Hayden implored Rachel.

She hadn't wanted to dance at all. "Well, I...."

Sam immediately took Rachel's arm in his hand. "She's promised all the dances to me, Hayden," he said, a little edgily.

Hayden cocked an eyebrow. "Surely just one?" he addressed her.

"I said *all*," Sam muttered as he urged Rachel forward.

Rachel looked at Hayden with a baffled smile.

The furniture had been removed from the drawing room and it had been transformed into a ballroom. Sam left Rachel to talk to the orchestra. He returned and immediately pulled Rachel into his arms.

"Let's dance," he said, moving to the music.

She tried to resist.

"Relax," he said, tightening his hold.

"Relax?" she asked, pulling a little harder. "What's wrong with you?" she whispered, drawing her brows together. "And what was all that back there with Hayden? I never promised any dance with you—much less *all* of them."

He refused to let go of her. "If you'll just relax, I'll explain," he said quietly.

She pressed her lips together in disapproval, then decided to stop resisting, and looked into his averted face, waiting to hear his answer.

"Well?"

Sam looked over her head, refusing to meet her eyes. "I'll tell you in a few moments. The dance floor is no place to talk about this."

"Talk about what?" she asked, bewildered.

"Shh. Be quiet and just enjoy the dance."

When her thoughts settled down, she became aware that with his arm about her, guiding her, she was dancing pretty well. She looked into his face and found he was watching her.

"You're—quite—good."

She had nearly said wonderful and felt a little embarrassed.

He didn't answer, but a smile touched the corners of his mouth.

When the dance ended, she expected to be led away to hear his explanation. But he claimed her again and again.

"Aren't they playing only waltzes?" questioned Rachel.

"Yes."

"I wonder why."

"I asked them to…at least for a while."

She smiled. He'd been thinking of her lack of dancing skills.

She began to tire. At the end of the set, Sam left to get refreshments, and Hayden, who'd been biding his time, hurried to Rachel's side.

Giving her a big smile as he approached, Hayden snatched up her hand. As he pressed it to his lips again, he murmured, "Mrs. Templeton."

"Mr. Spencer."

"Oh, Madam, aren't the proprieties so stuffy? Please...if it doesn't make you too uncomfortable, call me Hayden."

"All right...Hayden." She nodded uncertainly. "And—and you may call me Rachel," she said, suddenly a little shy. Hayden responded with a slight bow.

Releasing her hand, he asked, "If I may be so bold, Rachel...may I ask why you came with Sam tonight instead of your husband?"

She was surprised until she realized that not everyone knew her circumstances. Flustered, she answered, "Well, in the first place, I didn't really come with Sam—well, I did, but that was only because he had to pass my property on his way to town. So naturally, to be courteous, he offered me a ride. And in the second place, my husband was killed on our journey here to Stone Valley."

"Oh, my dear, Rachel, I am so sorry!"

"Yes...um...."

Rachel looked toward the refreshment table and saw that Claudia was trying her best to occupy Sam and a dart of jealousy went through her.

"What—what was that, Hayden?" bringing her attention back to what he was saying.

"I said, so you're not *really* here with Sam?" Hayden asked curiously.

"Well, yes and no." She studied her hands for a moment. "No. No...not really," she said decisively and looked at him with a brilliant smile.

"Hmm...." Hayden said. Glancing at Sam, he frowned slightly. "Well, it appears that Sam feels differently."

"Differently? I'm afraid I don't understand."

"Just look at him." Hayden laughed, leaning in towards her. "If you're not *really* with him, then I wonder why he's shooting daggers at me this moment. And those eyes of his are hungry…hungry for you."

She opened her mouth to disagree, but turning in the direction Hayden was looking, was startled by Sam's gaze on her as he stood across the room in conversation with Claudia. The look on his face was anything but pleasant. In fact, his frown was thunderous. Sam's eyes narrowed as he shifted his eyes to Hayden and pressed his lips into a tight line.

Sam was angry. Good and angry by the dark look he was giving her. Sam wasn't anything like Hayden described as far as she could see. He said Sam had hungry eyes. Cold, detached Sam had hungry eyes—for her? Impossible! Yet…she remembered their lunch at the restaurant. There was hunger in them then.

The room became overwhelmingly stuffy and Rachel felt the need to escape.

She asked, "I'd like some fresh air, Hayden. Would you mind?"

CHAPTER THIRTEEN

STANDING ON THE VERANDA, the air fragrant with the scent of an abundance of rose bushes shipped in from Virginia, Rachel vehemently denied that Sam had any feeling for her, but Hayden was adamant.

"Oh, but he does, dear lady," he informed her, baring his teeth in a grin. "Take my word for it."

"You're wrong about that, Hayden. Sam barely tolerates me," pausing as though in thought, "and for the life of me, I don't know why he doesn't like me," Rachel said.

With a half-laugh, Hayden replied, "Don't fool yourself." His eyes flickering with amusement, "He does."

"He does? Like me?" she asked, astonished. "Sam and I don't get along very well at all. We're always at odds," she said, moodily.

"I see." Hayden raised an eyebrow, "I think there's more than you're telling."

"I have nothing to tell. Except...."

"Go on."

"Except—well...." she didn't like talking to Sam's cousin about this. It felt somehow disloyal. In spite of her hesitation, she rushed on, "He has control over my entire life, if you must know."

His interest was piqued. "You mean, like blackmail?"

"What's blackmail?" she questioned, her inexperience clear on her face.

Stepping back a little, Hayden searched her face in the light from the window. Either she was teasing him or she had been totally sheltered in life.

"You don't know?"

"No," she answered honestly, looking up at him.

Leaning against the post, "Blackmail," Hayden patiently explained, "is when someone knows something bad about you, something you don't want others to know, and they try to extort something from you to keep silent about it."

"Oh. I see," Rachel said quietly. Sam knew about her divorce from Peter. He had told her that on the road to Kentucky. Could this be something he held over Ransom's head? Was the making of the will a result of that knowledge? It sounded far-fetched, and she doubted even Sam would go that far.

Rachel gave her head a little shake in denial. "No. Sam's not doing anything like that."

Hayden stood in silence, waiting for her to continue.

"My husband," Rachel reluctantly offered, "made a will before he died, giving Sam complete control over all my estate, including my money."

Opening her fan, she swished it a couple of times, then said: "I can hardly breathe without Sam's approval."

"Hmm," he expressed thoughtfully. "I seriously doubt the will has that much to do with Sam's actions. To me, it's as plain as day that Sam has feelings for you and the looks he threw at me prove it. So—are you going to do anything about it?"

"About what?"

"The will. Are you going to do something about the will?" Hayden repeated.

"The will? Me?" Rachel asked, incredulously. "What can I do about it?"

"Have you talked to another attorney?"

"What good would that do?" she asked a little helplessly. "The only other attorney in town is Tom McClelland...and he is friends with Sam."

He lifted one shoulder as the corners of his mouth turned down. "It might not do much good anyway."

"I figured as much," she responded, clearly discouraged.

"I studied law," Hayden revealed. Rachel perked up immediately, but her countenance fell when he added, "However, I'm not a licensed attorney.

"Perhaps there is some type of loophole," Hayden mused. "You have read the will, haven't you?"

"Yes...no," she corrected herself, shrugged her shoulders, and looked down.

"No?" Hayden asked, surprised.

"No...not really," she answered. "I mean, Sam pointed out some parts of it to me, but I've never really read the entire thing myself."

"Well," Hayden began, biting his upper lip in thought. "Perhaps there's some type of provision in the will that releases Sam from responsibility."

A glimmer of hope struck her and raising her head, she grew alert.

"Such as?"

"Oh—there could be any number of things," Hayden remarked, as he toyed with the freshly painted railing, "remarriage—or something such as that."

As the first real possibility of freedom dawned on her, Rachel looked at Hayden and decided right then and there, that he was an absolutely charming man and one that must truly be sent from God. She had a feeling their friendship was developing fast and as she said something to that effect, Hayden took her inside and danced another dance with her.

Her body wasn't the only thing whirling. Her mind spinning round and round. She decided, friend or no friend, she must see Tom McClelland tomorrow.

The ride home had Rachel's stomach upset. Sam was ominously silent. She had never seen him so angry before, not even when he found out about the lumber deal she had made. She was glad it was dark—somehow it might protect her. From just what, she didn't know.

Her eyes were shimmering with unshed tears and she really didn't know why. Rachel was bewildered by the fact that Sam could be so cold to her one moment and completely different the next. She turned her head away so he couldn't see as she brushed away the tears that threatened to spill over her cheeks.

Hayden offered to drive Rachel home, but Sam, like a cat with unsheathed claws, refused, in spite of Hayden's persistent protests. The contention was so sharp that Rachel feared, as did others who were standing nearby, that it might progress to fisticuffs. In fact, Oliver had to be summoned to settle the dispute.

"Hayden," Oliver had suggested, "it's only right that Sam take Rachel home. She came with him and it's on his way."

Hayden didn't like losing, especially to an old rival like Sam...even though they were cousins.

They had traveled about two miles in heavy silence and Rachel's nerves were stretched to their limit.

"I can't go on like this—I can't," thought Rachel, sitting in the buggy, skirt wadded in her hand, heart fluttering with anxiety. Glancing around at the deep woods, "I can't, I won't. I'll jump out of this buggy and run home. I don't care if it is dark!"

As though he read her mind, Sam shifted the reins to one hand as his other hand closed on her arm firmly, blocking any escape.

That was just what she needed. Her panic quickly dissipated as though his restraining hand had squeezed the last ounce of fear out of her, and anger took its place.

"Let go of me!" she cried as she tried to shake his hand from her.

"Not until you promise to stay in the buggy," Sam said, tightening his hold.

"I'd rather walk!" she declared.

"You're not walking," Sam said evenly, "not in the dark, anyway. I took you to the party and I'm seeing you home."

"I never asked you to take me to the party," Rachel uttered. "And Hayden offered to drive me home!"

"Well, yes, that's another matter," Sam calmly remarked.

"What do you mean?"

"Hayden."

"What about Hayden?" she curiously asked, relaxing a little.

He removed his hand from her arm and took the reins back in both hands. "There are a few things you need to know about him."

She looked at his face in the faint moonlight, her interest piquing. "Such as?"

"He's my cousin and...don't get me wrong...we get along quite well...."

"It didn't seem that way to me tonight," she interjected.

He grew quiet. They rode along in silence for several more minutes. The clop-clop of the horse's hooves relaxed Rachel and lulled her out of her agitation.

"Be careful of Hayden," Sam warned, giving Rachel a start as he broke the silence.

"What are you talking about?" Rachel sputtered. "What's wrong with Hayden?"

"Hayden is a ladies' man. He knows how to charm."

Pausing, "All too well, I might add."

Hayden did not seem to be a ladies' man to her. Rather, just the opposite. He seemed quite the gentleman. She didn't know what Sam's problem was, but she wished he would solve it.

"I've heard the same about you," she threw at him.

He laughed. "Well—that was true...at one time."

"What was true?" Rachel asked somewhat crossly, "the part about you being a ladies' man or the part that you could charm?"

"Oh, I can still charm," he said smoothly, "but I don't chase the ladies any longer."

She snorted. "Huh! You could have fooled me!" she uttered as she adjusted her skirt.

Sam turned to look at her stormy face. "What are you talking about?" he asked.

It wouldn't do to let him know that she was jealous of Claudia and she refused to discuss it any further.

The buggy hit a hole and pitched forward, throwing Rachel and Sam closer together. Feeling the brush of his coat against her bare arm, her heart began to thump as the skin on her arm tingled. Rachel ran her hand down her arm and shivered.

"Cold?" he asked.

She shook her head no. "It's just that—that—I forgot my wrap."

Sam reined the horse to a stop. He slipped off his coat and placed it around her shoulders, gently brushing her neckline in the process. She shivered again as goose-bumps traveled down her arms.

She lifted her face toward his and sat motionless for a few moments, staring into his eyes, her heart beginning to beat somewhat erratically. As his lips moved closer to hers, without thinking, she angled her head to receive his kiss.

But he didn't kiss her. Stopping short of the point of touch, Sam slowly withdrew his arm, turned, and picked up the reins. He chirruped to the horse and the buggy started rolling again.

She was disappointed.

CHAPTER FOURTEEN

THE NEXT MORNING, Sam was at New Wellington Inn bright and early, rapping on Hayden's door. There was no answer. Rapping again, Sam heard something fall on the floor. He knocked one more time and Hayden finally appeared, disheveled from sleep.

"Sam! What in the world are you doing here so early?" Hayden asked, running a hand through his sandy hair and wiping the sleep from his eyes. "It's barely sunrise."

Pushing past Hayden, Sam hastily entered the room and then turned on his heel.

"I'll get right to the point, Hayden," he stiffly said. "I want you to stay away from Rachel Templeton."

Hayden looked at Sam for a long moment. "Whatever for?" he incredulously asked.

"Don't give me that innocent act." Emotion flickered across Sam's face, jerking his lips and tightening his jaw. "You know what for. I know you, Hayden. We were both cut from the same cloth. Remember? I know your past and I won't have you trifling with Rachel."

"*You* won't have me...." Hayden threw back his head and laughed heartily as he closed the door behind him. "What's got into you, cousin? I've never seen you so worked up over a girl before."

"I'm *not* worked up," Sam denied as he changed his expression, but inside his heart was racing. His hands dropped to his sides. "I'm simply warning you... stay away."

Hayden cocked a brow at him. Sam couldn't fool him. He saw beyond the cool façade he was trying to project. The clenching of his jaw told Hayden there was more to it than Sam was letting on and he studied Sam curiously before replying.

"You know, cousin, I think you've got feelings for the little lady."

"That's not exactly true," argued Sam as he shifted on his feet.

Hayden crossed the room to the pitcher of water on the stand. Picking up the glass with one hand and the pitcher with the other, he asked calmly, "Well, then tell me, cousin. What *is* exactly the truth?"

"Rachel's just an acquaintance." Shaking his head, Sam admitted, "No. That's not quite true, either. She's my ward."

"Ward?" Hayden asked as he held the pitcher in midair. Turning to look at Sam, he asked with disbelief, "You mean you're Rachel's guardian?"

Sam jutted out his jaw. "Yes, it's something like that." Squaring his shoulders, "Yes, that's right. I'm her guardian," Sam emphatically answered.

Turning back to the pitcher and shrugging his shoulders as he filled the glass, Hayden commented, "Well, Sam, I just can't see you in a role like that."

"I don't suppose you can," Sam scathingly said. "Your vision is pretty short-sighted."

Hayden regarded him with amusement. "That isn't quite how Rachel tells it."

"What do you mean?"

Lifting the glass to his lips, Hayden watched Sam over the rim of the goblet.

"She said you have control over her finances, but that doesn't exactly make her your ward." Taking a long drink, he then added: "Remember, I studied law, too."

"It goes a little deeper than that," Sam said, and his eyes began to gleam oddly.

Setting the glass down, "Perhaps you would care to enlighten me," Hayden invited.

"No, I wouldn't," Sam replied, refusing to meet Hayden's eyes.

Hayden studied Sam, and then remarked: "This is a first for you. I've never seen you quite like this. You've never cared about anyone like you're acting about Rachel. Of course, I must say, she looks like a girl who could break a man's heart."

Wondering whether to elaborate any further, Hayden threw caution to the wind and asked, "Don't have any future plans for Rachel, yourself, do you?"

Sam stiffened for a moment, but decided to ignore his question. Hayden had hit a nerve. Those thoughts, indeed, had been meandering through his mind. But he strongly doubted that Rachel would agree, so deep was her resentment of his intrusion into her life.

"Rachel's been through a lot," Sam quietly said. "I just don't want to see her get hurt."

"Well, I don't know what she's been through. And knowing you, I suppose you won't tell me, either."

Hayden ran his tongue over his upper teeth. "What makes you think I want to hurt Rachel?"

Giving Hayden a skeptical look, Sam answered: "I know you, Hayden. You'll promise her the moon, and then drop her, leaving her devastated. Just as you have so many others. Remember the last girl you made love to? Look where she is today…in her grave."

Hayden frowned. "I take no responsibility for that. She wasn't quite emotionally stable, you know."

"That's just the point. You take no responsibility at all."

Hayden shrugged and gave Sam an airy wave.

Sam knew Hayden like no one else did. Trifling with girls' emotions had been competitive sport between them in the days before Sam had become a Christian. What Hayden did now was his own affair, but not where Rachel was concerned. He would fight him with everything he possessed and he knew it would take some doing to convince Rachel what Hayden really was.

"I don't want you to lead Rachel on," Sam told Hayden.

"I'm not leading her on," Hayden countered defensively. "I just want to get to know her."

"She doesn't know the difference." Agitated, Sam remarked, "I don't want you to break her heart."

"Really now, Sam!" Hayden replied, clearly bored with Sam's interrogation. "Rachel's not a child to be shielded from life. She's a grown woman…a widow, to boot."

Hayden sat down on the edge of the bed and studied his nails. "What if I was to tell you that I have no intention of breaking her heart?"

Sam's eyes narrowed. "What do you mean?" His stomach clenched tighter than it had already been.

"I feel quite drawn to Rachel, if you'd like to know," Hayden said. "She's different than other women."

Looking up, "I'm thinking seriously about courting her," he said with a crooked smile,

Taking a step toward Hayden, Sam growled, "Not without my consent, you won't."

Hayden rose quickly from the bed, his fists balled, ready to fight, eyes flashing.

"With or without your consent," he retorted. "You can't stop me. She's an adult with a mind of her own."

"She doesn't fit into the lifestyle that you live," informed Sam. "You move in different circles, with parties and the like. Rachel's a simple girl and used to living in the country. For your information, she doesn't even like parties."

The bed creaked from Hayden's weight as he plopped back down on it. "She seemed perfectly at ease last night. You could say," crowed Hayden, "that we got on quite well."

"That's because I was with her," said Sam. "She doesn't know your kind of world and could never adjust. She would never be happy away from North Star."

Hayden shrugged one shoulder as the corners of his mouth turned down. "I haven't thought ahead that far, yet," he confessed.

"No, you don't think much at all," Sam spoke, running his hand through his hair. "I'm warning you, Hayden, leave Rachel alone."

"No," Hayden answered, springing to his feet again. Giving Sam a questioning look, "that is, unless you have plans for her yourself. But then, come to think of it…that never stopped me before."

CHAPTER FIFTEEN

"TOM," SAID RACHEL, AS SHE PACED THE FLOOR, her arms hugging her body, "I need to know about Ransom's will."

Tom leaned back in the chair behind his desk until the front legs rose from the floor. His elbows were on the arms of the chair and his interlaced fingers rested under his chin.

"Rachel, I haven't seen it. Sam has it. You know that. Why didn't you go to him?"

Sighing, she stammered, "I—I wanted to come to you first."

Looking at her speculatively, "I don't think there's much I can do for you, Rachel. I've heard Sam has executor power over your estate."

"Exactly!" she blurted out, aggravated, as she stopped in front of his desk. Bending over and placing her palms on the desk, she said, "I need to know if there are any provisions in the will that allow me to get power over my own money. Not just when I'm twenty-five...but now!"

Tom and his wife Lacy had been at the party and saw the rift between Sam and Hayden. Searching Rachel's face, Tom wondered if it had anything to do with Ransom's will. No, in all likelihood, he concluded, it was over Rachel, herself.

Tom ran a finger over the bridge of his nose. "Let's see. Ransom has been dead nearly a year. This is July and Sam read the will—sometime last October, wasn't it?"

Rachel nodded.

"And you don't know what's in the will?"

She shook her head no.

"Haven't you read the will, Rachel?" Tom asked in surprise.

"Well—I—I," she sputtered, "Not exactly. I guess I was just so upset. Sam read different parts to me. I suppose I just took his word about it all. And to tell you the truth, I was so shocked to find out that Ransom had given Sam power over my finances that I don't recall much about it."

The chair's front legs hit the floor. Giving her an apologetic smile and throwing his hands wide, he told her, "Sorry, Rachel, the will is not in my hands and Sam will not share that information with me. What I suggest, if you really want to know, go to Sam to get the details. He's the one you should have gone to in the first place."

Rachel knew that already, she really did. But Sam had been jumpy as a cat last night and she didn't relish tangling with him today, not about something important as the will, especially after the near altercation between him and Hayden.

But she just had to know if there was any way out of her mess. If Hayden was right, her salvation from Sam was probably somewhere in the pages of that document in his office. Awake most of the night, she had hurried the dawn to break so that she might rush to town.

"But can't you ask him, Tom?" she wheedled. "He listens to you."

"Sorry again," shaking his head. "You're his client and I can't interfere."

Leaving Tom's office, "Why, oh why," she thought for the hundredth time, "did Ransom choose Sam instead of Tom?" She liked Tom. Tom's brother and sister-in-law were killed on the road, leaving him and his new bride Lacy to raise his brother's little son and daughter, Adam and Starr.

Smiling to herself, she thought that Tom would make a good father. He was easygoing, almost like the brother she had never had. If she'd ever had a sibling, she would have wanted him to be just like Tom. His soft brown eyes had a kind look for everyone and an ear ready to listen to one's troubles.

But Sam!

Gritting her teeth, she walked next door. Lifting her skirt and stepping up the step, she pushed open the door to Sam's law office, gearing herself to do battle. She wondered if Sam would even let her see the will, but her mind was made up. Either she would read it for herself or she would sue Sam.

Sam was sitting behind his desk, busily engrossed in a deed dispute. As Rachel, heels clicking rapidly, marched into his office, he half-rose and his chair scraped the floor.

Surprised to see her there, "You usually send Frank for supplies," Sam said, right to the point. "Is there something else you need to see me about?"

"Yes, there is." Drawing a breath, she demanded, "I want to see Ransom's will."

"Whatever for?" he asked, perplexed.

"It's my right." Crossing her arms, she said, "I haven't really read it and I want to do so now."

Studying her fiery eyes, without another word, Sam turned to the cabinet behind him. Going through the contents of a drawer, he finally located the will. He motioned for her to sit, sat down himself, and silently handed her the document.

Turning the pages, she read: *In the event that Rachel should remarry, Sam Spencer's executor power will cease. This provision is hereby contingent upon Sam Spencer's approval of Rachel's proposed marriage.*

She couldn't believe it! She could only have power over her own money if she were married again! And she had to have Sam's approval of the marriage, at that? That was like asking Pa for his permission! And Sam rarely approved of anything she did, much less marriage.

"This is too much to be borne!" she thought in a state of shock.

Rachel looked up wide-eyed and dumbfounded. She was trapped. There was no way out that she could see and the next approximately seven years were to be spent groveling to Sam Spencer. Her dark eyes began to flash anger.

Intently watching Rachel's face and every move she made, Sam was suddenly assaulted with flying pages thrown angrily at him.

Rachel struck the desk with her fist and stood so quickly that her chair jangled to the wooden floor.

"No!" she exploded, and then stormed out of the office, slamming the door behind her.

Tom saw her exit Sam's office, heading up the street like a pack of wild dogs were after her, and out of curiosity, dropped in.

Sam was putting the will back in order.

Tom grinned as he stood before the desk. "I see Rachel didn't like what she read."

"How did you know what she was doing in here?" Sam asked suspiciously.

"She stopped by my office first."

"Your office?" Sam asked, puzzled, as he nodded for Tom to sit. "What did she want with you?"

Righting the chair that Rachel, in her fury, had tossed back, then seating himself, "Oh," Tom said with amusement on his face, "she wanted me to investigate, on her behalf, just exactly what Ransom's will contains."

"What was she looking for, do you think?" Sam wanted to know.

"How to break the will," Tom bluntly stated.

"Well...you and I both know that's highly unlikely," Sam sardonically commented.

"Yes. Rachel mentioned something about gaining financial control when she turns twenty-five, though." Tom related.

Sam nodded. "That was Ransom's stipulation. But you know another thing that Rachel's probably not aware of?"

"What's that?" Tom asked curiously.

"There's that little law called the 'Law of Coverture' that states that when she remarries, all rights to her money and property go to her new husband. She won't be able to have control even then."

"You're right about that." Tom gave a wry grin. "Are you going to tell her?"

Sam grinned back. "Tell her? I don't think so. Not at this time, anyway. It's been hard enough dealing with her as it is. Rachel would really be angry if she was aware of that little bit of information."

With an air of gravity, Sam continued, "I'll tell you one thing, though. I'm going to have to keep an eye on whomever she gets involved with...and one person in particular.

"Hayden?" Tom asked.

Sam nodded. "Yes. He knows about that law and I'm afraid he's playing her for a fool. Yet, if I was to tell her, she wouldn't believe me. Hayden would make sure of that."

CHAPTER SIXTEEN

"YOU'RE DIFFERENT THAN YOU WERE A COUPLE OF YEARS AGO," Oliver told Sam. They were sitting in the café and had just given their order to the waiter.

"How's that, Father?"

Oliver smiled at him indulgently. "You've got your feet on the ground now, and you're more cautious."

"Well, as far as the cautious part, I don't know if that's good or bad."

"Oh...to be sure, son, it's a good thing."

"Perhaps."

"I had wondered if you would ever straighten up your life. And look at you now! Attorney, minister, and soon to be district judge."

"I have to admit—I owe it all to God. I found out there was more to life than being the life of the party and pursuing women."

"Yes. You know, I've been watching you. I believe for the first time you may have fallen in love, son," Oliver said as his eyes twinkled. "At first, I had wondered if it was Claudia Stone that had thrown an influencing shadow over you. But now, I have the sneaking suspicion it's that young lady, Rachel. I've seen the way you look at her."

Sam drew a deep breath and lines creased his forehead. "I don't know, Father. You may be right. But I seriously doubt that she's in love with me. To be perfectly honest, we argue all the time. No...let me correct that. *She* argues. Most of the time, I play defense. Rachel's very strong-minded and refuses to listen to reason."

Oliver laughed. "That's just it. You're used to young ladies who have no opinions of their own, whatsoever. That's partly the reason why you became disillusioned with them. You've found one now who stands up to you and you're a little unsure how to deal with her." With a sparkle in his eye, Oliver asked, "Or should I say...intrigued?"

Sam gave a little laugh. "I think I could find a way to deal with her, but Ransom's will keeps her up in arms all the time."

He rubbed his forehead. "She views me as the enemy and resents the fact that I have power over her money and estate and she doggedly keeps playing that same tune all the time. And I'm worried. You know how Hayden is.... I know," as he held up his hand in defense, "because I was the same way."

Oliver nodded.

Sam drew a deep sigh. "I desperately need your advice, Father. And I'm going to tell you some things about Rachel, but I don't want Hayden to know."

Oliver thought for a moment and then promised.

"Rachel was raised in seclusion by her mother and father. Her father signed Rachel to Jacob and Elizabeth Templeton as their ward. Their son, Ransom, fell in love with Rachel, but in all honesty, I don't think she felt as strongly as he.

"Long story short, Ransom went away to university and Rachel met someone else and married him. He turned out to be a notorious gambler who wanted her farm to sell and abused her. When he found out Jacob Templeton had legal authority over her farm, this man left. She moved back to her farm and—uh—er—had some further difficulties.

"When Ransom came home from the university, he moved her back in with Reverend Templeton. She then learned that her husband had divorced her. A week later, she and Ransom were married. They began their journey here to New Wellington but he died in an accident on the way. After he was dead, she found that she was going to have his baby."

"Oh, my!" Oliver exclaimed.

"And that is pretty much where she stands today. Except—that Ransom had made a will, naming me executor over all her affairs."

"Hmm," Oliver voiced. "That's a lot for anyone to go through, especially a young woman. By the way, how old is she now?"

"Nearly eighteen."

Oliver clucked his tongue while shaking his head in pity. "I've met her father, John Winslow, but where's her mother?"

"She died nearly three years ago."

"Too bad."

"But there's more," Sam added.

"More?" Oliver asked, amazed.

"I forfeit power of attorney on the day that she remarries."

"Well...that seems pretty straightforward to me."

"Well, it's not. Ransom also stipulated that this provision was contingent upon the fact that I approve of the marriage."

Oliver stared at Sam. "And how does Rachel feel about that?"

"That's just it," he said, throwing up his hands. "She's pretty much in a rage over it."

"I can understand why," Oliver acknowledged. "That would be hard for anyone to take."

"Hayden has let me know that he is going to court Rachel. You know his reputation, Father. And you know that I could never approve of such an engagement."

Oliver scratched behind his ear and asked, "How do you know that Rachel agrees to his courting her?"

"Father," Sam sighed, "Rachel is so naïve. She believes everything anyone tells her and has made some very bad decisions, particularly where men are concerned."

"So you're saying you are trying to protect her because of the will?"

"Partly."

"And?" Oliver asked, probing a little deeper into Sam's feelings. "What's the other part?"

Sam felt a little uncomfortable revealing his feelings and it showed. "Umm...there's just something about her, Father. Not only do I want to comply with the will...but I...of my own volition, want to protect her...take care of her. Do you understand what I'm saying?"

"I think I'm beginning to. Now...I'll ask you again. Are you in love with Rachel?"

"Yes," Sam finally admitted. Fretfully, he added, "But I don't have much of a chance with Hayden flitting around her."

Oliver hated to see his son in such a state. True, Sam had been up to his neck in careless emotional schemes in the past, but a definite change had come over him. And Oliver liked the change.

If need be, Oliver would cut the visit short and return to Virginia, taking Hayden with him, if it would help gain Sam his unfulfilled dream. "Well, son, take my word for it," Oliver encouraged, "I think you have more of a chance than you realize."

Sam searched Oliver's eyes for some clue about the situation. "Is there something you know that I don't, Father?"

116

Oliver smiled an easy smile. "Sometimes, love and hate seem to be very close to one another. I've seen how Rachel looks at you." With a half-nod and wave of his hand, "I know she resents your control, but Rachel's wrestling with her own emotions and if you weren't the executor, I suspect she might just surrender to you. It's a matter of pride with her. Give it some time and I'm sure she'll come around."

"I hope so," Sam answered, doubt coloring his voice.

Oliver nodded. "Have faith, my boy."

Sam eased back in his seat and for the first time realized how tense he had been. Everything about Rachel put him on edge, even talking to his father about her. However, his father's easy manner and astute judgment gave him a little more confidence about the situation. Plus...having someone to talk to about this helped to ease his mind tremendously.

"I had a long talk with Hayden," Sam confessed.

"About?"

"Rachel—of course."

"It's best to clear the air about these things," Oliver advised.

"Hayden didn't take kindly to my 'clearing the air'. He seems pretty serious about pursuing Rachel." Glancing down and toying with his silverware, he said, "I really believe for the first time that he's got marriage on his mind."

Pursing his lips, he looked up and said, "But, Father, Rachel wouldn't be happy married to him. She's pretty much connected with the earth and loves her estate at North Star and I told him so."

"Well, son, no matter what Hayden has said, he's still pretty much a ladies' man. I doubt seriously if he'll change any time soon." Oliver gave Sam another wave of his hand, "Oh, I know. Hayden's told me the same thing. He's declared that he's madly in love with her. And I imagine he really thinks he is."

"You know Hayden and I have been close in the past. There's a difference in the way he talks about Rachel," Sam gravely said.

Oliver grew thoughtful. A small smile curved his lips. "Don't just sit back and let Hayden move in. Stake your claim. You used to know how."

Hearing the kitchen door creak open, Sam laughed a self-deprecating laugh as he glanced past his father to the waiter bringing their food. "I still do. But there's the little matter of the will standing in the way."

Sitting in his cabin that evening, Sam gazed at the fireplace, the flames slowly turning into dying embers. It had begun to shower and as the rain fell on the roof, and the wind blew in the open cabin window, the tallow candle on the mantle sputtered and went out.

The storm had cooled the night and throwing another log on the fire and closing the shutters, he settled back down into the chair.

"Well, I've done it," he thought, relaxing before the fire's hypnotic flame. "I've finally admitted that I'm in love with Rachel. And it took my father to worm it out of me. But I guess I've known down deep that I've loved her all along."

With this realization came the peace he had been missing or rather the missing piece of his life. "I suppose there's a kind of life I've wanted—looked for and been afraid of—afraid of trying for."

Though Rachel was already twice-married, Sam sensed marriage had passed over her without touching any deep chord within her. She had married Peter in hopes of moving back to her farm and married Ransom to get out of Wellington.

He had to give her credit. After getting into a fix about the lumber for her house, she was smart enough to find a way out of it and now her dream of a fine home was starting to unfold before her.

But Sam had his own dream…a dream gaining momentum…like the flames rising from the fresh log in the fireplace. "With everything within me, I intend on making that dream come true," Sam decided. "I am going to marry Rachel Templeton."

He smiled to himself. "She just doesn't know it…yet."

CHAPTER SEVENTEEN

THE MORNING AFTER THE PARTY, Jane was furious when Will finally returned home.

"Where have you been, Will?" she demanded.

He ran a hand over his haggard face. "Some equipment broke down at the mill. I spent the night fixing it."

"You couldn't make it home for our first real party?" asked Jane.

"Sorry, Jane. I am backed up on orders and I had to get things running again."

"Didn't you know how significant that party was? How important to have in our home a congressman such as Oliver Spencer? You know very well that Jacob wants to put someone into politics to represent Kentucky. If you're not careful, it just may very well be Sam or Tom and not you."

"Jane, at this point," Will tiredly said, "I don't care who gets into politics. I'm not sure I'm the right man for political affairs, anyway. I have my own plans."

"Oh, of course," she spat at him, "*your* plans. What about me and what *I* want? I'm warning you, Will, you'd better not mess this up for me. I came to this God-forsaken place against my better judgment, and you'd better make it worth my while. I gave up being with my parents in Wellington, and, if I'm going to be stuck out here, I, at least, want you to climb up the political ladder to success."

Will looked into Jane's eyes and felt nothing. He had forged ahead in life always growing, flexing, pursuing new opportunities, always seeing each day as filled with new adventures and challenges. In each situation he grew, whereas Jane had somehow remained unaffected by the experiences of life, never looking beyond herself to what could be except as to how it might feather her cap.

"Can our marriage be saved?" he thought. "What is left between us that can be salvaged?"

Will walked away silently toward their bedroom, away from her incessant nagging. He pushed open the door to the children's playroom. There was a glad cry in Jake's high-pitched voice.

"Daddy, where have you been?"

Will picked him up and whirled him around, then hugged him tight. Yes, if there was anything at all, it was Jake and Beth. They were two very good reasons for staying.

"Can you believe it, Cissa?" Jane was furious as she rose and began pacing the room. "Will couldn't find time to attend the party we were giving for the Spencers'. At his very own home, no less! Think about it! A congressman! I have plans for our future. Will knew all about that. I've talked to him extensively about getting into politics. And he deliberately missed the party!"

"Well, Jane, Will did have business to attend to," Cissa answered. "He couldn't help it. He told you that."

Overlooking Cissa's defense of Will, Jane went on, "I'm so angry, I'm thinking about taking Jake and Beth and going back home to Virginia!"

"It's too dangerous for you to travel all that way by yourself! You know what a difficult time we had coming here over the road."

"I've been checking." Jane was pacing the floor again, deep in thought, her hand cupping her chin. "We can travel the Ohio. It's not nearly as dangerous now as before."

"But, Jane! Surely you can find it in your heart to stay and work things out with Will."

"No!" she cried, throwing her arms to her sides. "I've tried and tried. I'm always giving and he's always taking."

"Can't you think of the reasons you fell in love with Will? Can he have changed that much from when you first met him?"

They had grown up together, Jane and Will. They went to the same church, same social functions, same school, and he had teased her as she tried to tag along, calling her Plain Jane.

She never gave him much thought in her childhood beyond the fact that he was Reverend Templeton's eldest son, but since that day four years ago, when he was newly home from the university, she had loved him...loved everything about him, including his quick wit and driving energy.

His first Sunday back to church, as she sat with her family in their pew, second from the front, even now, she could recall every detail of what he was wearing as he sat proudly on the platform with his father, and how his eyes, with surprised recognition, caught hers. From that day, she wanted him and was swept along in his enthusiasm as he pursued her until she said yes. But now, with sadness, she realized that she had been just another of his pursuits, and once they were married, the conquest over, she was relegated to the leftovers of his time.

"No, I suppose he hasn't really changed," Jane admitted as she grasped the back of the chair. "I just never saw it coming. Will swept me up in the passion of the moment and I thought it would go on forever. Now I can see that I'm just a possession to him, something he never finds time for. He feels that same way about everything in life...always looking for some fresh new challenge. Never satisfied with what he has."

"Will is a unique individual," placated Cissa. "God has given him the talent and ability to make things happen. Just look at all he has accomplished in this town and in such a short time, too. Why, practically everyone here owes their own success to Will. Look at all the shops that have opened. James told me that Will has plans for a gristmill and for mining salt. You know how important salt is. He could be very rich someday. And think about your children. They need their father.

"Humph!" exclaimed Jane. "They may need him, but they rarely see him!"

Cissa sighed. "I certainly can't tell you what to do, Jane, but I will tell you that Will is still the same person now as when you first met him. He has a good heart and I know he loves you."

Jane shook her head violently. "I never wanted to come here in the first place and I was a fool to do so. I should have returned to Wellington after our first day out.

"What you may not know, Cissa, is that Will offered to send me back after our first day of leaving Wellington. He didn't even try to convince me to stay with the party. Now, do you want to tell me that's love?"

"You must have misunderstood him, Jane."

"It's no use, Cissa," Jane said, shaking her head again. "I just can't see it working out for us anymore."

It was settled. On a crystal-clear morning, Jane had readied the children, and after finally discarding many of the things she'd wanted to take with her, packed a few clothes and other essentials, along with provisions to last several days, she had the servants to load them in the buggy.

She was leaving. No longer content with an absentee husband, the time had come to bid farewell to her majestic home and travel back to Wellington, Virginia. Back to where her father Jules and mother Katharine were. Jane had thought about it long and hard. The fact that the trip must be made without Will to help her was finally laid to rest. She could make it. She knew she could. They would travel to the Falls and board a boat from there headed for Virginia.

Overhearing the servants whisper that morning, she warned them that Will was not to know, nor anyone else. Not one single person. Not Jacob or Elizabeth Templeton, James, or Cissa.

As she climbed into the buggy and took the reins, there were no tears. That time was over. Starting a new life on her own would be a formidable feat, but it could be done and do it she would. She was tired of pleading with Will to pay attention to her, and her mind was made up. It was now or never.

Glancing one last time at the house, her pride and a status symbol in the town, she then turned and drove off, leaving behind her past, looking forward to a new future.

After the town had disappeared from view, as she was heading toward Mission Point, Jane passed by North Star. Seeing Rachel's new house in progress did little to stir any feelings within her. Jane had never really cared much for Rachel. She never considered Rachel to be in her class. She was too wild and uninhibited for her taste. But she could see from a distance that it would be a grand home. "A home like Ransom wanted," Rachel had told her.

Wrenching her eyes away and concentrating on the road ahead, "Let her have her country life! I'm going back to civilization!"

Will arrived home after midnight, and finding the house dark, lit the lamp and wandered from room to room searching for his family. Finding no one, he went to Jacob's and was told they had not been there.

Exasperated, he decided to stop by their servant's home. Roused from sleep, Nancy appeared at the door, clutching her wrapper about her, her husband hovering behind her.

"No, sir! She's been gone all day," was her explanation. Nancy didn't ask him in and stood peering from behind the half-open door.

"When was the last time you saw her?" he asked.

"It was early this morning, sir—right after breakfast."

"And she's been gone all day?"

"Yes, sir, all day."

"She didn't say where she was going?" asked Will.

"No. She didn't tell me."

"And she took the children?"

She nodded.

"Did she pack any clothes?"

Nancy looked down and moved her big toe in a circle on the floor.

"I suppose I could tell you that," she said reluctantly. "Yes, she did."

"And you don't know where she went?"

Nancy shook her head, "No, sir. I don't have any idea."

Will said, "Thanks," and left.

Wracking his mind as he walked away, he concluded that there was only one place she could have gone and that was back to

Virginia. "Crazy girl—how did she think she could ever make that trip alone—and with two children, at that?"

Riding in the dark toward Mission Point, it dawned on him how unhappy Jane must be if she would make such a journey on her own. He had listened to her complain and whine about his absence from home for so long that it had become easy to tune her out and go about his business. He never dreamed she would actually go through with her threats.

In Virginia, it would have been a different story. Her parents, who lived close by, were always willing to take her in and he never had to worry about her. In fact, he had left her once and stayed with his own parents when they were having one of their disagreements. Their arguments had been so bitter at times.

Still, he was able to have more time for Jane there and take it easier, for Wellington was a town already established. He merely filled his niche.

But New Wellington—that was different. The townspeople here relied on him for nearly everything. Lumber to build their homes, organizing the town, helping to get businesses into operation, keeping a steady shipment of supplies coming in from the Falls, and a thousand other things.

In the few precious moments he had for quiet time with God, usually early in the morning at the lumber mill before the workers arrived, he felt riddled with guilt because he no longer had time for ministry. Not only was he letting God down, but his father, too. And Jane bristled at him because she wanted him to succeed in politics! Where did she think he would ever find the time?

Hearing the clop-clop of his horse's hooves echo in the dark woods, Will prayed, "God, I don't know what move to make next. I love my family and want to be a good husband and father, but without your help, I simply don't know how."

As though God's voice spoke to his heart, he heard, "What would happen if some of the things you wanted done for the day were left undone?"

After thinking for a few moments, *Some* of the things? "Nothing," he finally surmised.

That got him to thinking. God was right. When he came to the end of his life, ready to draw his last breath, he wouldn't be worrying about all the things he never completed. But it did frighten him a little that the most important task, ministry, had been neglected. Yes, things had to change and, more importantly, his way of thinking. Perhaps he couldn't change Jane, but he could change himself.

Will half-smiled in the darkness. He sent up a plea, "Help me to set my priorities in order," and clucked to the horse, urging it to go faster, faster, to Jane and his children.

CHAPTER EIGHTEEN

"DO YOU HAVE A ROOM YOU CAN PUT US IN FOR THE NIGHT?" Jane asked Jubal Munday, owner of the tavern at Mission Point.

Jubal studied the trio standing before him. Jane, waiting impatiently for an answer, was holding Beth in her arms as Jake held to her skirts, peeking out at Jubal with an affectionate grin.

"You have room for us for the night?" Jane asked again, a little irritated.

Jubal spat tobacco juice at the spittoon, missing it by six inches, where the stained floor was a silent witness to past misses.

"Are you alone, little lady?" Jubal asked, wiping his mouth with the back of his hand.

"Yes—yes, we are," Jane answered, beginning to feel uncomfortable.

"Where you all headed?"

"We're going to the Falls of the Ohio and from there, to Virginia."

"Then you're coming *from* New Wellington?" Jubal asked, skeptically.

"Yes."

"And you've got no man with you?" he asked, warily.

"Correct…there is no man with me."

As though that is any concern of his.

"Well…most folks go *to* New Wellington, not away from it."

"Please, Mr. Munday. Do you or do you not have a room you can put us in?"

Jubal hiked a thumb over his shoulder. "I've got a room back there. It's not much. But you're welcome to it."

"Fine. How much do I owe you, Mr. Munday?" Jane asked with all the politeness she could muster.

Jubal smiled a yellow-toothed grin that was missing an eyetooth.

"Ma'am—if someone such as yourself has got the gumption to travel this wilderness alone, then I say to you, there's no charge."

Jane lay on the rope bed, Beth sleeping beside her and Jake at her feet, his little arm thrown across her ankle. It was stifling in the windowless room and unable to sleep, Jane decided to leave the children there while she went out for some air. Listening for their even breathing and then disentangling herself from Jake's grasp and nudging him over, she crept outside and settled on a split log made into a bench.

A sleeping dog near the door of the tavern came awake, raised his head, wagged his tail slowly, and gave a little sound in anticipation of companionship. Thinking better of it, the shaggy mutt lay his head back down and went back to sleep.

An owl hooted. Jane looked up at the sliver of moon that was shining. There were no lights anywhere else as everyone in Mission Point was asleep. Jane could barely make out the few cabins dotting the hillside in the settlement, which, when she arrived, had poured forth entire families to see the stranger that had come among them.

A scrubby lot they were, dirty and poorly dressed. Clutching her children closer to her, she had cringed at the settlers' touch, refusing their overtures of friendliness and rushed into the tavern. Jubal Munday was surprised to see her stumble through the door, wide-eyed as though a bear was after her.

And then there was that little Indian boy, the one with the blue eyes. He studied her without ever uttering a word. What a strange lot they were!

Pulling her skirt up over her knees, Jane lifted the hem and fanned herself, creating a little swishing of the still, hot air, blowing the damp tendrils of her hair. Her arms ached from tugging the reins all day and she missed her comfortable bed.

Rubbing her hand across her eyes, she was weary. "I suppose Will is home by now," she thought. He was rarely home before ten o'clock at night, usually long after she and the children were settled in bed. Swatting at a mosquito, she wondered what he was doing and if he was thinking about her.

Melancholy swept over her. Away from her home in New Wellington and traveling in uncertain country, Jane had never felt so alone in her entire life. Even the trip here to Kentucky, as hard as it was, did not compare to what she felt now. At least on the road, there was the entire party traveling together.

Now, there was no one. Thinking of Jake and Beth, she wondered if she had done the best thing for them. They could become sick or be killed by Indians with no one to protect them. She hadn't even thought to bring a pistol with her and this morning's courage began to wane in the light of reality.

Oh! How foolish she had been! But if she went back now, Will would probably laugh at her and living with him would be absolutely unbearable. She spent most of the next hour debating whether to go back or to continue on.

The air outside didn't feel much cooler than it had in the room, and Jane knew she should go back where the children slept in case they woke and cried for her. But the idea of returning to that filthy, stuffy place revolted her and she couldn't go back. Not just yet.

Leaning her head back against the cabin, her back cramping with weariness, "At least, I know Mother and Father are concerned about me. Will certainly is not!" she grumbled in the dark to herself.

The dog roused again at the sound of her voice, waited, and then lay his head back down again.

"I suppose I should do the same," Jane thought as she looked at the mutt. "Hashing over the situation is not doing me any good, and I need some sleep."

Dropping the hem and drawing her skirt over her knees, she stood up, stepped around the bench, pushed open the door, and went to bed.

Will arrived at Mission Point just as dawn was breaking.

Entering the tavern and looking around, "Hello," he said "Is anyone here?"

In a few moments, Jane appeared, holding Beth while Jake waddled in crying, "Daddy!" Toddling over to Will, Jake grabbed hold of Will's trousers. Picking Jake up, Will pressed him to his chest as though he would never let him go.

For a few awkward moments, Will and Jane stood staring at each other. Jane had never seen him look so tired. Had she been so unhappy that she had never really noticed before? She knew he had been working hard…too hard.

Her heart skipped a beat and Jane realized she really did love him. And in that instant, she knew this was what she had been waiting for. She wanted him there, with her, for her, only her.

"Jane," Will asked, "Can we talk outside?" Jane had never seen Will this uncertain before and it felt rather strange. It seemed as if for the first time in a very long time, they would have a real conversation. This should have elated her. But it didn't. It humbled her.

Jubal ambled from his room, yawning and rubbing his hair. "Morning," he said to no one in particular.

"Good morning, Jubal," Will answered, giving him a nod.

Jubal stopped, looked long at Will, and ventured, "Don't I know you? Didn't you come through here with the caravan almost a year ago?"

Will gave his head another nod. "Yes, that's right. I'm Will Templeton."

"Right, right," Jubal said, turning towards the bar. "I remember now. You're some kind of kin to John Winslow."

"Well, sort of indirectly. John's daughter was married to my youngest brother."

"Was?" Jubal questioned.

"Yes. My brother was killed on our journey here."

Jubal pursed his lips in thought for a few moments.

"That must have been the trouble that John didn't want to talk about," Jubal commented more to himself than to Will.

"Daddy," Jake said in his piping little voice, "I'm hungwy."

"If you folks will wait a spell, I'll roust you up some breakfast," Jubal offered.

"Billy!" Jubal called to the Indian boy who appeared in the doorway. "Go find a few eggs to feed these folks. And tell Mamie Dane we need some fresh milk."

Quick as a wink, Billy was out the door.

"If you don't mind, Jubal," Will said, "I'd like to talk to my wife outside while we're waiting."

132

Throwing a knowing look at Jane, Jubal smirked a little and said, "Sure thing, Templeton. Take your time. Take all the time you need."

Will and Jane were conversing by the buggy when Billy passed by, carrying eggs and a bucket of milk. Gingerly juggling the half-dozen eggs in one arm and the bucket in the other, Billy commented when Will came to the rescue, "Should have brought a basket."

After depositing the eggs inside, Will appeared again and approached the buggy. "Let's go sit under the shade tree, Jane."

Taking the baby and helping Jane to the grass, Will sat across from her. She hadn't had time to tidy up since he arrived, and since he was usually gone in the morning before she awoke and arrived home well after dark, it had been a long time since he had seen her hair flowing, tousled from sleep, around her face. The rare moments they were together in the waking hours found her meticulously groomed. He liked her like this. Soft and natural, as when they were first reacquainted in his father's church.

"You were saying, Will?" Jane asked.

"Yes, of course." After clearing his throat, he said, "I know it's been a difficult time for you, Jane. And I realize I've been extremely busy."

She watched his face and decided to remain quiet for the present. After all, he knew how she felt, had known for a long time. She had told him often enough and in as many ways as she could find.

Beth was crawling off Will's lap, attempting to reach the grass. Bending one knee, keeping his foot flat on the ground, and hooking the other foot around his ankle, he lifted her up and set her down in the crook of his lap.

"I've been too busy, as you know well—too busy for you, for Jake and Beth, and even for God." There was a pained expression on his face that went straight to Jane's heart.

"It's just that people have depended on me so to get New Wellington settled, and I've just made myself too accessible. I see that now. It was just too easy to ignore you when everyone else was clamoring for my time. I felt you'd always be there. Be there when I needed you. I never thought you'd really leave. I'm asking you to help me. I need to set new priorities. I know that not only do I have a responsibility toward you, but also to Jake and Beth."

He had bared his heart to her, she saw that. That was something he had not done in a very long time. Something in his honesty touched her heart. She realized she needed to change too—needed to be kinder and more loving.

Suddenly, she was afraid. It was easy when she could shift all the blame to Will, but now that he was willing to change, she instinctively knew she would forever be the shrew in the town's eyes if she did not respond in kind. She had nagged and whined for so long that she wondered if she could truly mend her ways.

Unsure of herself, she finally spoke. "I—I know that things have not been right between us for a long time. And I'm not sure how well we'll do at all this changing that needs to happen," she commented with a half-laugh. "But if you're willing, then I'm willing to give it a try." She ran her tongue over her upper teeth and pressed her lips together. "Will, I'm afraid. What if we don't make it?"

Will searched her eyes for a few moments then smiled an easy smile. "Relax," he cajoled. "Aren't you married to the eternal optimist?"

His smile was contagious and it felt good. This was the old Will she had known. Smiling back, Jane merely nodded her head.

Reaching out to touch her hand, he said, "There's something I'm going to let you know. I wasn't going to tell you just yet. I was saving the surprise for your birthday in September."

Puzzled, Jane cocked her head sideways at him. "What surprise? You've given me just about everything anyone could want."

Pleased with himself, he said, "I know how much you've missed your mother and father and I've been secretly corresponding with them. They have agreed to sell their property holdings and move here to New Wellington. They should arrive here in time for your birthday."

Shocked, her mouth flew open and she sputtered, "Mother—Father—moving here—to New Wellington?"

"Yes. Are you pleased with your surprise?"

"But they never wrote me about it."

"Like I said, it's a surprise."

Tears filled her eyes and began to slip down her cheeks. Quickly rising to her knees, she threw herself against Will, wrapping her arms about his neck and Beth sent up a wail in the crush.

Sobbing, Jane cried out, "Pleased? Oh, Will—this means all the world to me."

Raising her head to look at him, she said as plans were already formulating in her mind, "And we've got enough room. They can move in with us."

He lifted a hand. "That won't be necessary, Jane. I've already started building their house and, believe me, your parents will be satisfied with it. And it's close by ours."

Jubal's voice sounded out the door. "Breakfast," he called.

"Thank you, Will!" Jane said. If there was anything at all she could do for him, she would try her best, from this day forward.

CHAPTER NINETEEN

THE FOLLOWING MONDAY, Rachel managed to put all thoughts of Sam Spencer out of her head and focus on the new shipment that had arrived. Everything from bolts of cloth to salt had been transported from the Falls and Rachel was busily sorting through crates when Hayden walked through the door.

Looking up from her bent-over position, her face lit up at the sight of him. Tucking a strand of hair that had slipped from a pinned-up curl, she brushed imaginary dust from her bodice as he approached.

"Good morning, Rachel—or should I say my dear Mrs. Templeton?" he bowed theatrically as he removed his hat.

Her cheeks blushing a pretty pink, she giggled, "Please Hayden—or—should I say Mr. Spencer?"

He laughed heartily, which made her laugh.

"Oh, Hayden!"

"Come with me today," Hayden urged.

"Goodness! Where to?"

"Anywhere. You name it, dear lady," he cajoled. "A buggy ride, a picnic, a stroll about town."

"I couldn't possibly leave the store. I have all this work to do."

"Which reminds me, why are you working in Templeton Store when you have your own estate to look after?"

Rachel sighed. "It's a long story. I can't tell you here."

"Then come with me," Hayden said, holding out a hand to her, "and inform me."

Rachel shook her head and drew back, turning back to the crate. "I told you, I can't."

"There's other help here," he reasoned, leaning in toward her. "They can take over for you."

"I know they can," she said lifting small sacks of salt from the crate. Walking toward the counter, she deposited the bags on it. Turning and sweeping back her hair, she walked back to the crate for more. "But I have an obligation to Will," she remarked. "I can't just go running off any time I feel like it. I have responsibilities."

At that precise moment, Will walked in. Rachel and Hayden, deep in conversation caught his eye, and he wondered if the stranger was the Hayden Spencer he'd heard about, as the news of the near skirmish between Hayden and Sam had quickly traveled through the town.

When Jane finally settled down from her temper tantrum about him missing the party, it was the first piece of gossip she told him. The men at the mill had also heard about it and hee-hawed about the near incident at the fancy do.

Though Will never paid much attention to that kind of gossip, he noticed Rachel's face was flushed, and her eyes unusually lit and sparkling.

"Good morning, Will!" Rachel called, lifting two more sacks.

"Rachel," he nodded somberly and walked toward them.

"Will, I don't think you've met Hayden Spencer. He is Sam's cousin."

"No, I haven't," Will answered as he shook Hayden's hand. "I had to miss the party the other night," he apologetically offered.

"Hayden Spencer, Will Templeton."

"Pleasure's all mine, Mr. Templeton," Hayden nodded. Smiling indulgently at Rachel, he continued, "I was trying to persuade Mrs. Templeton to come for a buggy ride with me this morning. But she insists that she's much too busy."

"Mr. Spencer's right," she said as she walked to the counter and deposited the sacks. "I'm very busy."

Since she'd admitted her deception about the lumber, she had fast become one of Will's favorite people. He valued honesty in people and she was a great worker…conscientious to a fault. He felt guilty in a way about her working in the store. She should be home with her baby, but try as hard as he could to convince her, she wouldn't have it any other way. As she said, "the debt must be paid."

It would probably do her some good to take a break. Looking on half-amused and half-apprehensive, he answered thoughtfully, "Of course, if Rachel would like to take off for a few hours, that would be fine."

"Are you sure, Will?" Rachel questioned. He seemed a little too quick to let her out of work.

"Yes, of course."

Rachel paused. She didn't like letting Will down, especially since he'd been so good to her.

"Go ahead," he said, smiling his lopsided smile, taking the sacks from her and walking toward the counter. Calling over his shoulder, "But remember, Mother is expecting you for dinner. Six o'clock sharp."

Rachel stood for a moment watching his retreating back. Finally, taking off her apron, she allowed Hayden to lead her to the door. As she turned back to give Will some instructions about the supplies, he waved her on.

"Go. Have a good time."

And with that, they walked out the door.

Will didn't approve of Rachel going with Hayden without a chaperon. But who was he to tell a twice-married woman what to do?

Dinner at the Templeton home turned out to be a surprise for Rachel. Hayden had neglected to inform her that Sam, Oliver, and he, had been invited, also.

Hayden was made much of by Elizabeth, who insisted he sit at Rachel's right hand. Between adoring looks and conversation from Hayden and glares from Sam, sitting across the table, Rachel would have been hard-pressed to recall what was served at the dinner table.

Trying to relieve the pressure she was feeling, she concentrated on the wonderful early afternoon she'd spent with Hayden. Winding up at Ezzel's Creek, sitting under an oak tree amidst the blooming wildflowers, Rachel found in Hayden someone who was comfortable as an old shoe. Time had slipped rapidly away as he regaled her with jokes, anecdotes, and stories about the capital city.

"Now," Hayden had announced, turning the conversation to her. "Suppose you tell me what all the mystery is about you working at Templeton Store."

Rachel readjusted her skirt and prepared to explain her dilemma.

"As you know, Sam has control over my finances."

He nodded.

"My husband, Ransom, had a dream of building a fine home on our estate at North Star. But, unfortunately, he was killed on our way here. So, I asked Sam if I could buy lumber for the house, and he said 'no'. While Sam made a trip to Virginia, I talked Will into giving me the lumber.

"Well...of course, you know Sam. When he returned, he was furious and demanded that I find a way to pay Will. I had no other skills, so I convinced Will to let me work off the debt at Templeton Store." Rachel looked at Hayden and said: "And that's that."

"Hmm," Hayden uttered thoughtfully. "It was a little mean of Sam to insist that you pay for the lumber."

Rachel shrugged. "Well, mean or not...he did."

"I've never met a woman quite like you," Hayden remarked smoothly, suddenly changing the tack of the conversation.

Rachel raised her eyebrows. "I'm no different from any other woman."

"Yes, you are—for me, anyway. You have integrity, you're resourceful, and I'm happy to say...very pretty."

"Pretty?" Rachel looked at him skeptically. Sam didn't think she was pretty. But it was obvious to her that he thought Claudia was. Everyone talked about them and hinted that they would marry, even though Sam always insisted there was only friendship between them.

Hayden reached out suddenly and took her hand.

Surprised, she looked at him, and he said, "I think I'm falling in love with you, Rachel," and kissed her fingertips.

Shock ran through her at his familiarity and declaration. She quickly pulled her hand away. "Please don't do that again, Hayden," Rachel remonstrated.

"I might," he smiled. "Would you be angry if I told you that you are the most beautiful woman I've ever met and I admire you very much?"

"It will do you no good," she answered with a half-laugh.

In his eyes a tiny light flickered like a small flame. "I know that. I just wanted you to know."

Lost in the reverie of the afternoon, she hardly heard a word anyone was saying at dinner. Her nails tracing a line over her lower lip, she met Hayden's eyes and blushed unexpectedly like a child caught in the honey jar.

The moment was not lost on Sam and as though a force was drawing her, she turned slightly and found his eyes intently searching her face. Her blush deepened and her gaze faltered before his scrutiny.

Hayden, noticing the exchange, shot a triumphant look at Sam and redoubled his efforts to engage Rachel in conversation.

Rachel managed to get through the next hour by making small talk about the store, Abigail and Gabe's upcoming wedding, and the weather. Relieved, when the dinner was over, she feigned weariness, and pleaded to be excused.

"I'll see you home," Sam immediately told her.

Hayden opened his mouth to offer her his company, but Sam, scraping back his chair as he rose, cut him off and said, "It's on my way."

Sam had purchased his own buggy and, amid Rachel's protests, he helped her into it. Retrieving Rachel's horse and tying him up to the back, Sam climbed in beside her.

"Never mind about taking me home, I can see my own way," Rachel said as Sam picked up the reins.

Chirruping to the horse, he stated, "*I'm* taking you home."

Rachel struggled to keep her voice calm. "Don't bother," she said, reaching toward the reins.

"No bother," he said, his hand brushing hers aside.

"But, I'd rather you didn't."

"Now, let's don't start that again, Rachel," declared Sam. "I said I'm taking you home."

She slumped back against the seat in frustrated resignation. He was always pushing her around, telling her what to do. What she wanted never mattered to him.

He practically raced the buggy to the edge of town, his face looking set and absent, as though he had forgotten where he was. Turning onto Ivy Street, they careened past the livery, and when they reached the edge of town that led to North Star, he finally drew up the reins a little. A brooding look was on his face.

CHAPTER TWENTY

IN THE HOT SUMMER TWILIGHT, the silence between Sam and Rachel was not a comfortable one and the tension was as sharp as shards of glass beneath their feet. It had been such a pleasant day spending lunch and the afternoon with Hayden, but now the look on Sam's face had her stomach tied in knots again.

It was difficult to relax with Sam, for just what he expected of her, Rachel had no idea. Though she had grown very fond of him, she never knew what mood to anticipate next. She watched as his hands tightly clutched the reins as though he was struggling with something and it frightened her a little.

He sensed her anxiety and willed himself to calm down.

"You didn't have to leave the dinner, you know," Rachel finally ventured, "especially with your father there."

"No problem," he said abruptly. "I'll see him tomorrow."

"Why can't I buy my own buggy?" Rachel asked. "That way, you wouldn't have to bother seeing me home all the time."

"I feel better about your safety if I know your whereabouts," Sam told her. "Besides," he said softly, "I like seeing you home."

Startled at his confession, something in his voice made her heart beat a little faster, but Rachel remained silent and confused.

"As you've probably guessed, I've been spending quite a lot of time with my father lately."

She nodded. "Yes, I'd heard."

"What you may not have heard is that I'll probably be appointed judge for this district."

Rachel gave him a studied look in the fading light. "That's quite a feather in your cap. I thought Jacob was considering having you appointed to congress."

"He was. He was," Sam nodded. "That's what Father and Jacob were planning to do, but I decided I didn't want to spend so much time away from New Wellington." *From you,* Sam meant. "My services can best be used right here. And since an active minister is not allowed to serve in the legislature, I want to stay involved in ministry."

"Will you have time for that?" she questioned doubtfully. "It appears you're busy enough now. You know—with your estate, law practice, and ministry." She wanted to add "and me," but kept her mouth shut on that.

"Indeed. But you know a busy person is the person who usually gets the job done."

No, she didn't know that. She started to analyze what he'd said, but quickly shut it from her mind. Rachel needed time to think.

Sam had become so intertwined in her life that at times it almost seemed as though they were married. Those weren't her thoughts exactly. Hayden had said those very words to her today. Trying to see her alone was becoming difficult and Hayden was like a bull pawing the ground, ready to charge Sam.

Perhaps if she could use Sam's new position as judge to ease him out of her personal life, he would leave her alone and allow her to see who she wanted and when.

"I've spent so much time with my father as of late," Sam interrupted her thoughts, "I haven't been able to make it to North Star for a few days. Are there any problems there? How are the livestock doing?"

"Fine," she answered and went back to her thoughts again.

"And your help?"

"Um? Oh, yes. Caleb and his sons are doing a magnificent job. You don't know how pleased I am when I ride in at the end of the day and find some new transformation has taken place. And Mary...."

Silence.

Sam looked at her quizzically, but said nothing.

"Sam," Rachel finally spoke.

"Yes?"

"I—um—we need to get something settled," she began nervously.

"What's that?"

"Well...seeing that you're going to be so busy with this added responsibility of becoming judge," clearing her throat, she continued, "and you and I know that Ransom made...uh...certain stipulations in the will concerning me."

A growing suspicion that she was leading up to some idea that he would not agree with took root instantly, and warily, he asked, "And?"

Rachel twiddled her fingers nervously before answering, her head bowed toward them, yet not seeing them. "It's just that—I—I want to release you from whatever other responsibility you feel you have toward me."

There. She'd finally said it and she relaxed.

"Do you want to clarify that statement?" asked Sam, guardedly.

Taking a little breath and blowing it out again, "I'm free to come and go as I please, am I not?" she asked.

"Yes," he nodded cautiously and slowly.

"And I'm free to choose my own friends, am I not?"

"You can choose your friends as long as they have your best interest at heart," he informed her.

"Then I don't need you to squire me around."

"Yes, you do," he argued, shaking his head.

"No, I don't," she bristled. "I can take care of myself."

He looked at her briefly with a twinkle in his eyes as a smile touched the corners of his lips. "Rachel, don't ever say that to a man whether you think that or not."

"And why not," she said, looking at his profile, "may I ask?"

"The rules of etiquette say that a lady should never tell a man she can take care of herself."

"Bah!" she declared, clearly unconvinced. She turned back to the road before them. "I've never cared much for 'rules of etiquette'. Why, just ask Elizabeth Templeton. She'll tell you—."

Her face turned crimson and she clapped her hand over her mouth, realizing what she had just said. How could she, Rachel Templeton, openly admit to such a thing! And to Sam Spencer, of all people! It was true she didn't necessarily like the rules that townspeople always imposed, but she had spent a great deal of time worrying about what people thought of her and emulating them...at least trying to, anyway.

He laughed. "You're quite the little rebel," he teased softly. He leaned closer to her and his voice filled with amusement, "The rebel with snapping black eyes."

Taking her hand away from her mouth, she drew herself to her fullest, trying to regain some composure. "Now why on earth would you say that?" she asked with studied coolness.

"You're always defying convention. Always have, always will."

"I'm sure I don't know what you mean," she denied with all the coldness she could muster.

"You like to do things your way, no matter what's right or wrong."

"That's not true!" declared Rachel. "I always want to do what's right!"

"No?" he asked. "Just think back on the last couple of years."

He had her there. She had defied the citizens of Wellington by going to the lumber mill and wearing britches, among a number of other things. But no matter how many wrong decisions she had made, she still wanted to do the right thing. It was just what others considered right did not always seem right to her.

"I don't think you understand me, Sam."

"How's that?"

"I was raised to do what I wanted, when I wanted, and all the rules that other people put on me strangle me sometimes."

"Don't let what I said bother you, Rachel," he said with amusement. "I like your frankness. Pretentious women have never held any charms for me."

Rachel was sure she held no charms for Sam, either—frankness or otherwise.

"Back to my original statement," Sam said with a soft, chuckling laugh, "never let a man know that you don't need him."

"Hogwash! Why should I act any differently than what I feel?"

"Because. It makes a man feel important when he can protect his lady—uh—when he can protect women."

Somewhere in her mind, a bell of recognition rang. Suddenly, Rachel was back in Wellington, Virginia, standing in Jane's kitchen. Jane's words were as clear in her ears, echoing that thought, as though it was she and not Sam who was speaking.

"Jane said something like that to me once," Rachel thoughtfully replied.

"What was that?" he asked sharply, all ears.

"She said that we have to appear helpless in order to become betrothed. I asked why and she said it makes men feel strong, like they're the protector."

"What else did she say?"

"She said we're taught to obtain our identity through a man. So I said, 'You're saying that I can't be what I am—I have to pretend to be what a man thinks'?"

Rachel paused.

"Go on," he said, interested.

"She said yes."

"And...what did you say?"

"I said, 'If that is what it takes to get married, I just won't bother'."

Sam threw back his head and laughed until he nearly choked. "That's what I'm trying to tell you," he said after catching his breath. "Here you are, not quite eighteen and married twice already with virtually no effort on your part, while other girls are trying desperately to catch even one husband. You've got a mind of your own," rubbing his cheek, he continued, "and I daresay that I have felt the brunt of your words time and time again."

A smile covered his whole face. "Yes, Rachel...you are quite the little rebel."

"Rebel or not," she said in annoyance, jerking the ribbon on her hat, unsettling it and reaching up to right it again, she retorted, "I like to take care of myself."

"That may be what you want," Sam said, instantly sobered, "but I made a solemn promise to Ransom that I would care for you and give you my protection."

Oh! The vow he made at Ransom's death is causing me all kind of trouble!

Hayden was in the picture now and she resented Sam's interference in her personal life. It was one thing to control her finances, but quite another to control which friends she chose.

"And what if I don't want your care and protection?" she haughtily asked.

"Nevertheless," Sam said, setting his eyes straight ahead, "you've got it."

CHAPTER TWENTY-ONE

THE DATE FOR THE MARRIAGE OF Abigail Newgate and Gabe Roswell had finally been set, and the whole town closed shop to attend the wedding. The small lawn beside the church wasn't roomy enough for the reception, and as the large crowd spilled into the street, makeshift tables were set up on the dusty lane to accommodate the gathering.

Every crystal glass in town had been borrowed and never had Rachel seen a more splendid buffet. Elizabeth outdid herself this time. Overseeing the food, she was in her element, giving orders to the ladies working the tables.

Noon came and the sun was high and hot, and not a breath of air stirred the leaves.

Other than Tom and Lacy's wedding at the Anderson Blockhouse, the only other wedding Rachel had attended had been James and Cissa's, excluding her own marriages, of course. But hers had both been small affairs, with only the family in attendance at the parsonage.

Abigail had looked splendid dressed in brown brocade and Gabe had never looked happier. They would make a good marriage. Everyone said so.

Rachel frowned as she thought of her own ceremonies in Virginia. Both times the church folk never approved…especially her marriage to Ransom. He was the darling of the community. Handsome, of good character, and the most sought after bachelor for eligible young ladies. When the church received the news that he was to marry the divorced Rachel Brogade…well, it shocked the town. But marry her he did, and took her away to Kentucky.

A little sigh escaped her lips as she looked at the newly married couple. "This is the way it should be, she thought—a joyous day, full of celebration and not doom and gloom." She felt a little envious and a part of her wished that she could find that kind of happiness

Hayden left Rachel and worked his way across the packed street to get some refreshment for them.

Drifting through the music and gaiety, suddenly, behind her, as she opened her fan to cool herself, Rachel heard a voice that was all too familiar. A deep-timbered voice she would never forget as long as she lived. Her fan stopped in midair and her spine stiffened as her face drained of color.

As she stared at the crowd before her, listening to the tinkling of glass and the swell of laughter, that voice carried her unwillingly back to a time when she was held under lock and key by Peter Brogade.

A prisoner of her own husband, his mocking laugh and abusive behavior had its intended effect. Intimidation…and fear for her life. But she had lived and escaped, and after the divorce, Rachel thought she'd never see him again. Thought that when she walked out of that room they shared at the inn and back into the Templeton home almost two years ago, that he was gone out of her life forever.

Now Peter Brogade was here of all places! Here in Stone Valley—in New Wellington, where she was making a fresh start. Her past had followed her! Her past—that in spite of countless hours of agony—countless hours of struggling to forget—countless hours of wrestling with the notion that people silently disdained her because of her divorce...had come back to haunt her.

Sam, standing nearby with Claudia, caught the look on Rachel's face, and excused himself to go to her.

Reaching the edge of the crowd where Rachel was waiting for Hayden to return, Sam touched Rachel's shoulder and she swung about, back rigid, and her eyes were dark, haunted pools in the whiteness of her face.

"What is it, Rachel?" Sam asked.

She laid a hand, feverish and urgent, upon his arm. Concerned, his hand covered hers.

The eyes she turned on him reminded him of a rabbit caught in a trap. Panic filled them as she stared at him, mutely asking him to help her.

"Rachel?" he asked again, lowering his head closer to her face.

Cold little currents of fear that started in the pit of her stomach, flowed outward until the fingers that were hidden beneath Sam's warm hand, were ice-cold. In her armpits suddenly appeared the nervous stickiness of sweat. As beads of perspiration trickled down her sides, though the day was hot, Rachel felt a chill.

Looking into Sam's apprehensive face, for a few moments she could not speak.

Then: "It's Peter!" she finally croaked. She barely recognized the sound that erupted from her throat as her own.

"Peter?" Sam, drawing his brows together, asked. He hadn't noticed any strangers among the crowd and took a quick glance around.

Bending his face down toward hers again, he asked, "Here?"

Raising her eyes with a desperate plea to the heavens, Rachel nodded. Then she squeezed her eyes shut and prayed, *Lord, I'm going to need your help with this. I don't think I can make it through without it.*

"Peter Brogade?" he questioned again. "Your ex-husband?"

When she opened her eyes and nodded again, Sam asked, "Where?"

"Behind me—somewhere back there," she whispered frantically, leaning into him as her other hand, fan crushed in her grasp, clutched his forearm. "I recognized his voice. There's no mistake. I'd know that voice anywhere. It's Peter!"

Sam glanced behind Rachel and saw the tall stranger with black hair and close-clipped mustache, and determined that he must have just arrived. In conversation with Hayden, Peter looked Rachel's way as Hayden, hands carrying glasses full of liquid, jerked his head in her direction.

"Would you like to leave, Rachel?" Sam asked quietly.

Yes, she would. With all her heart, she would. But her feet were like lead. Though she willed them to move, they did not respond.

"My dear, Rachel!" sounded Peter's laughing voice behind her. "My very, dear, Rachel."

As he came face to face with her, with Hayden alongside, Rachel looked frantically around. Anywhere, except into Peter's eyes.

"Excuse us," Sam spoke, starting to pull Rachel away. "We were just leaving."

"Leaving? Just when I've finally found my wife?" he asked with surprise.

Rachel suddenly found her voice. "Ex-wife," she clarified quickly—too quickly.

Displaying even, white teeth, he flashed a smile. Laying his hand on his chest and making a slight bow, he said, "Pardon me—just an error of speech."

Hayden stood quietly by as the words flying between them electrified the air.

"What are you doing here, Peter?" she sarcastically asked, finally gaining some gumption. "Have you run out of saloons?"

"My, my, what a snit we're in today!" Peter sneered and drew on his cigar. Blowing the smoke, he said, "I did leave South Carolina only a few weeks ago. I spent some time in Charleston—very profitable time. I was preparing to make my way to Logan County when I heard you were living here now."

"How did you hear that?"

"Oh...I have my sources."

"What sources?"

"Let's just say, 'a mutual acquaintance'."

"A mutual acquaintance? Who would that be?"

"It doesn't really matter, does it?"

"And? Your plans?" Rachel asked.

"Oh, I thought I might just stick around a while. I'm kind of thinking about taking up residence on some land here."

"You?" asked Rachel incredulously. "What do you want with land? You're no farmer."

"Ah, you remember all too well." Looking down at his cigar and flicking the ashes, he said, "No. I'm not interested in farming. As a matter of fact, I'm thinking about starting a gaming hall."

"A gaming hall? Here? In Stone Valley?" she cried in disbelief.

He shrugged his shoulders as the corners of his mouth turned down. "One place is as good as another. Besides, I've heard the gambling places in Logan County are very numerous now. Not much room for competition. And if I start one here, I'll probably draw some customers from there. New territory—everyone's looking for new territory."

"This area doesn't want such activities going on here," Sam remonstrated.

"Um...could be. But just think about all the business it could bring into the town."

"We don't want that sort of business. We'll form a committee to keep you out of this area," Sam warned.

Peter crossed his arms and widened his stance. "You can't protest if I decide to acquire unoccupied land. By the way," Peter asked, looking Sam square in the eye, "who are you?"

Glancing down at the possessive way Sam's hand covered Rachel's, "Surely you haven't taken yourself a new husband, have you, Rachel?"

Rachel immediately tugged at her hand in Sam's tight grasp, "Sam is not my husband," she mumbled helplessly, looking as if she wished she were dead as she tried again without success to pull her hand free.

Sam's face was thunderous. "I'm Attorney Sam Spencer," he replied, refusing to release her hand, "and I'm on the Council of New Wellington...soon to be appointed judge for this district."

Peter pursed his lips and eyed Sam suspiciously, taking no pains to hide his arrogance, and then looked again at his cigar.

"Well, Sam Spencer," he finally drawled, "Councilman of New Wellington, and soon to be district judge—I wouldn't count your chickens before they hatch."

With that said, Peter spat on the ground, turned and walked away into the crowd. When he was gone, reaction set in and Rachel began shaking uncontrollably.

Suddenly aware of the people around her listening to the exchange of words, the day that had started as beautiful, was now becoming reminiscent of bygone days.

Rachel was mortified. She wasn't married to Peter anymore and his presence here shouldn't cast a dark shadow over her life now. But it did.

Sam whisked Rachel away, half-dragging and half-leading her to his office on the square. The plaza was empty for everyone was at the party. With one arm holding her up and the other fumbling in his pocket, he found the key, unlocked the door, swung it open, and handed her in.

The dim room swam with humid July heat and, almost instantly, drops of sweat began trailing down her arms. Closing the door, Sam moved to the window and after opening it, walked to a small sideboard where a crock of water stood, intending on dipping a cup for her to drink.

Exhausted mentally and emotionally from her encounter with Peter, Rachel put her head in her hands and began to cry.

Sam set the cup down, came up from behind and rubbed her clammy arms. "Rachel! Please!" he pleaded. "The last thing I want to see is you so upset."

Sam was used to women's tears. The Lord only knew how many tears he had caused to fall down lovely young faces as he had broken their hearts without a smidgen of regret in game-playing.

But he couldn't stand *her* tears and it was tearing him apart. She'd been so strong through everything she had gone through. Rachel had been the little rebel against devastating circumstances, never defeated and always rebounding, no matter what befell her. But beneath that tough exterior, she was crumbling, and he wanted to pick up every piece that fell and mend it carefully back together again.

She leaned her head against his shoulder and closed her eyes. A shock went through him as she did so. He had never held her like this before and it felt so right. More right than anything he'd done in a long, long time.

He wrapped his arms across her shoulders and held her tightly, murmuring soothing words against her hair. Her hand reached up and embraced his arm as tears of fright splashed down on her wrist.

At last, she pushed his arms away and turned to lean against his chest, wrapping her arms around his waist as though he was her last lifeline. He buried his lips in her hair, murmuring her name. Pulling her closer, all Sam could think was, "I've wanted to do this for so long. I didn't fully realize it until now, but now I know."

"Oh, Sam!" she exclaimed, encouraging his embrace, drawing strength from it. Lifting her tear-streaked face towards his, she knew in an instant by the look on his face, that he was going to kiss her—knew it as sure as anything.

But she couldn't let that happen, not yet, not here, not like this. Not out of pity for her or his vow to Ransom to look after her. If he had any feeling for her at all, it must stem from heartfelt emotion, not sympathy or obligation. She would not have it any other way.

Rachel drew back, dashed her hand across her wet eyes, and gave Sam a sidelong glance. For the first time since she had met him a year ago, he was no longer the aloof attorney, but was showing real passion toward her and she was at a loss as to how to respond.

His blue eyes traveled to her swollen lips, and he leaned in to kiss her. In those eyes were naked emotion, eyes that held no contempt, no scorn, no disapproval, just...should she think it? Love? No, no. She must be wrong. His eyes held her searching ones, eyes that said, "I love you."

She stepped back, looked away, and then looked back again, trying to understand what she was seeing.

"Please," she asked in a small voice, "may I have some water?"

CHAPTER TWENTY-TWO

RACHEL LIVED WITH IT BY DAY and took it to bed with her at night, lying awake in the warm darkness, her heart heavy and frightened, dreading the fact that Peter intended on taking up residence in Stone Valley. Her body longed for rest, but her mind wouldn't be still. Even Hayden's light-hearted presence, which had become a harmless diversion for her, couldn't completely alleviate her dismay.

Of all times for Peter to show up—just when her life was coming together at last! Frank and the servants were building her new home, and what should have been an exciting time for her was overshadowed by Peter's unwelcome presence.

Peter appeared at the store, offering to drive her home. No, not really offering. More like demanding. By some strange coincidence, Sam showed up just as Peter's request had turned into insistence. And when Hayden emerged a few seconds later through the door, black-brewing clouds threatened more than words.

Rachel breathed more easily knowing that Sam was near and intervening on her behalf, but she nevertheless yearned to have the ordeal over with. Longed for Peter to be gone and out of her life once again.

"Sam!" Rachel exclaimed. "Peter's got me so upset. I can't sleep. Truly, I'm afraid of him," she confided on their way home.

His eyes flickered with amusement. "I'd back you against Peter any day."

"You would?" she asked, surprised.

"I've always admired your spirit. No one can keep you down for long."

"But Peter is different," she admitted as she dipped her head. "You don't really know what he's like."

"I've seen enough like him," he said, frowning. "He's a tyrant."

Then he smiled at her and touched her hand. "You don't have to be afraid." Sam tried to be light about it, but she read the concern in his eyes. She smiled weakly in return, his touch unraveling the knot in the pit of her stomach.

Watching him from the corner of her eye, she marveled at Sam's transformation—so different from the Sam on the road who was indifferent. Just what brought about the change in him had her baffled. Maybe he was in love with her, after all, yet he certainly had not uttered those words to her.

Laughing inwardly, attributing the thought to her imagination, she doubted it was love. She had learned not to be presumptuous when it came to him, for he certainly lived up to his nickname, "Slippery Sam".

"Oh, well," she thought with a shrug. "Maybe I'll figure it out someday."

As Peter Brogade cavorted about town, flashing money, the upstanding citizens of New Wellington were all abuzz with the news that the notorious gambler had plans to erect a gaming hall outside of the town limits. Gathering at the newly constructed town hall, councilmen called a meeting, where the agitated citizenry demanded something be done to bring a halt to the unsavory plans that would ruin their entire community.

The tension was sharp. As the Council delayed, contention gained momentum and ran through the crowd gathered there.

Jumping to her feet, "What can we do about this?" Abigail Roswell demanded as soon as the meeting had been called to order. "I have schoolchildren to think about…and to have this kind of shenanigans going on…practically at our front door!"

Tom rose to address the litigious crowd. Raising his hands in an effort to bring order, "Well, folks. There's not really a whole lot we can do about it. People all over have taken to squatting and legally we, as a town, can't do much. It will have to be up to the state to decide. If Mr. Brogade decides to take up residence, we can't interfere. The Council has been talking about sending a delegation to the state capitol. But you must understand it takes time to get laws passed."

In the back of the room someone shouted out, "Why don't you become a congressman, Sam? Your family has experience in political matters."

As Tom took his seat, Sam rose. "I know there's been talk about making me a member of the legislature, but Kentucky's 1792 constitution excludes practicing ministers from serving as an elected representative."

"Then why don't you get out of ministry and go serve at the state?"

He half-smiled at that remark. Get out of ministry, indeed! "I understand how you think that I could benefit New Wellington if I did make such a decision. But this is my town and I feel I can be of service, not only in ministry, but here, locally, in our district in other ways."

"If you really cared about our town, you would," someone shouted.

Sunday morning dawned, and after sleep had evaded her most of the night, Rachel decided this would be the day to confront Peter.

Sam, Oliver, and Hayden had been invited by Elizabeth to Sunday dinner. For Rachel, getting Hayden alone was no easy task, as Sam's ever-watchful eyes were alert whenever Hayden was near.

Finding Sam engaged in conversation with Jacob and Oliver, Rachel motioned Hayden to follow her outside. Rounding the corner of the house and stopping beneath the crape myrtles, she spoke in a guarded whisper of her plans. She wanted Hayden to go with her to the New Wellington Inn where Peter was staying.

"I don't think that's a good idea, Rachel," Hayden quietly disagreed..

"But don't you see, Hayden?" she pleaded. "I may be the only one Peter will listen to."

"If you're banking on the fact that you were married to him, I doubt if he would give that any consideration at all."

"I believe he will," she argued.

Hayden shook his head. "I think it's too dangerous, Rachel. You don't know what the man will do."

"Exactly," she agreed. "That's why I want you to go with me."

"It appears that Peter Brogade will not listen to anyone or anything except the flash of currency."

"Please, Hayden?" she asked as she looked up at him imploringly. "Don't you know I need you?"

His willpower was wilting. He knew he shouldn't, but she was hard to resist, especially, when those dark eyes looked at him so enticingly.

"Well," began Hayden, uncertainty coloring his voice.

Seeing signs of weakening, she pressed him urgently, "If you'll go with me today, I promise I'll go anywhere you want—picnic or whatever. Just name it."

"Rachel, you know Sam will have my hide."

"Please, Hayden...just this once. Won't you, darling?" she asked, fluttering her eyes and laying her hand on his arm.

"If Sam finds out, he'll have a fit all right," he laughed half-heartedly. "It serves him right, though."

He paused in thought for a few seconds. She had called him 'darling'. "All right, I'll go." he finally told her.

CHAPTER TWENTY-THREE

AFTER CLIMBING THE STAIRS and entering a long, dark, hallway lit by a single lamp, they arrived at Peter's room.

Nearly losing her courage, Rachel paused for a long moment.

Charles, the desk clerk, had the impertinence to ask her why she wanted Brogade's room number. She had a hard time explaining just exactly what she was doing here and thought, "It'll be all over town before this day is out that I was consorting with such a scoundrel as Peter, and in his room, at that! My reputation may be ruined, but I must see him!"

Then, raising a fist toward the door, she whispered anxiously to Hayden, who was standing out of sight of the doorway, "Wait here," and knocked three short raps.

There was movement in the room and a few hesitant steps approached the other side of the door. The key turned in the lock and Peter pulled the door open a crack.

His look turned quickly to surprise and opening the door wide, he remarked, "Why, Rachel! You're the last person I expected to see."

Stepping back with a slight, mocking bow, he swept his arm toward the interior of the room. "Do come in."

Her stomach balled into knots at the sight of his dark, swarthy face. For about five seconds Rachel considered running back down the hall, but she was on a self-imposed mission to get rid of this man. Drawing a breath and extracting courage from a place beyond her shaking legs, she crossed the threshold and stepped into the room, careful to keep her skirts from brushing against Peter.

She looked quickly around. The room offered little. A window overlooking the street, a bed, a chair, a dressing table with a mirror, and on the table beneath the mirror a bowl and pitcher of water and the inevitable bottle of liquor.

Closing the door, Peter leaned his back onto it and gave her a long, appreciative look. She had matured. Her manner of dress and coiffure showed it. She was no longer the simple girl he had married two years ago, and the sight of her stirred a few things inside him, reminding him they were still there.

"And to what do I owe the pleasure of your company?" he asked, a smirking chortle in his voice. "On our last meeting you—er—didn't seem so—shall we say—eager to see me."

Hands clenched into fists and turning quickly on her heel to face him, "I came to ask you to leave town, Peter," Rachel hurriedly asked. She grimaced. She hadn't meant to blurt it out this way. Intending to reason with him, she had practiced her little speech all through the night, but the sight of him caused her to forget all her preplanned speeches and lose all poise.

His dark eyes danced as though amused by her request and discomposure. "That fact has been made quite clear already," he laughed as he pushed away from the door. "By quite a number of people, I might add."

His laugh unsettled her and made her long to push him backward or through the window or anywhere, for that matter. She hated him...hated his ill-timed laughter...hated his swarthy good looks. And most of all, she hated him for being in New Wellington...her town.

"Can't you see?" she implored, spreading her hands wide while ignoring his motion for her to sit in the chair. "The people of this town don't want you here. There's no place for your ki—" Trying to regain her composure, she finished, "for you."

"And you?" he asked, folding his arms with studied calmness. "What about you, Rachel? Do you want me to leave, too?"

"Yes!" she blurted out. "I want you to leave, too."

She turned her eyes to look at anything other than Peter's eyes. He was quiet. Rachel drew a long breath of relief as hope soared within her. Now that he knew how she felt, maybe he would leave town without delay.

"Surely you're not so naïve as to think that just by coming here and asking, that I would succumb to such a request? Do you honestly think I can be swayed by your—er—charms like the other men you know?"

Rachel was silent as hope dissipated like vapor.

What in the world ever made me think that Peter would listen to me, of all people?

"Trying to get rid of me like you did before, Rachel?" he questioned, narrowing his eyes.

His sudden shift surprised her and she stammered in puzzlement, "What—what on earth do you mean—like before?"

Peter unfolded his arms and casually walked to the table. Picking up the decanter, his muscled arms strained his shirt as he poured himself a drink. He was in excellent physical shape, and his good looks had always drawn admiring looks from women. They never knew how dangerous he could be. But she did…from personal experience. Every move he made, she was taking stock of him. He could change in an instant and she had never been very good at guessing what he might do.

With the glass poised in midair and swinging his upper body around, Peter looked at her. "You know exactly what I mean, Rachel. You left me in Wellington and went back to the Templeton household."

He was bringing that up—now? As though he had nothing whatsoever to do with her leaving?

Rachel, beside herself, fumed, "It wasn't working out between us, Peter. You know that. I didn't want to live at the inn. I wanted to go home to my farm. You—you had a different lifestyle than what I wanted. I didn't know that before we married. And remember…I didn't divorce you—just the opposite. You divorced me," she said, pointing her thumb to her chest.

"But you were the one who left," he accused icily, then turned and bolted the amber liquid.

Watching him tip his head back and drink, brought back memories. Memories she tried to forget. Memories…of being kept under lock and key, until he finally arrived at the inn in the middle of the night, inebriated. Memories…of marks left by his hands in the course of his angry tirades, memories…that swirled around in her head and left her heart cold, prompting her to finally utter, "You were abusive to me and only wanted my farm to sell."

Setting down the glass and brushing his mustache with the back of his hand, he shrugged as though what she said had no significance.

"I don't like losing," he said simply. "And when you walked out on me, it made me angry."

Peter took a cigar out of a box. After passing it slowly under his nostrils, he leaned over and lit it by drawing the flame from the burning lamp. Blowing out the smoke, and giving Rachel a once-over, Peter fixed his eyes on her turbulent face and calmly said, "I always knew there was something between you and Ransom."

Before she could consider that statement more than a heartbeat, "There was not!" she hotly denied as her chest heaved up and down. "Nothing had ever happened between Ransom and me!"

"You married him, didn't you?" he asked coolly.

She turned her head away from him and refused to answer.

"Look at me!" he demanded. "And don't give me any of your excuses."

Bringing her head up again, Rachel beheld eyes as cold as the freeze of winter.

"Again," he said, a hint of acid in his voice, "you married him, didn't you?"

As he drew on the cigar again, she paused before the jealousy in his eyes. "Yes, of course that's true, but—"

"My point exactly," he said, blowing out the smoke, his anger struggling to subside. He gained self-control again quickly enough, but there was still veiled fury in his eyes. He was unreasonable and she couldn't make him understand.

"Well..." Rachel ventured slowly, "I did eventually find out that Ransom loved me."

"Good," said Peter at last, "finally the truth."

"But that was after our divorce," she explained fretfully. "Ransom had never told me that he loved me before that. And that's a fact," she protested.

His eyes wandered over her face, lingering on her mouth. "Tell me this: when you received the news of our divorce, how long did you wait before you remarried?"

Rachel squirmed at his question and her eyes shifted toward the open window. The lace panel moved slightly as a small current of hot air blew in. Moving toward the window, she pulled aside the curtain and looked down at Main Street and the few inhabitants milling around.

How could she tell him that she married Ransom to get out of Wellington? Peter would never understand the stigma she had endured from the divorce. It didn't matter so much for a man, but a divorced woman was considered a disgrace and the town had crucified her for it.

"How long, Rachel?" he asked from behind her.

"One week," she murmured at last, nearly too quietly to be heard.

Peter stared at her back. "I see," he finally said.

No, you don't see! What's the use of even arguing with you? You'll never understand.

Bowing her head and then giving it a slight shake, "That's in the past, Peter," Rachel said with a trace of resignation in her voice. "Ransom's dead and I've started a new life here."

He shrugged nonchalantly. "That may be, but I'm staying."

Wrenching her head up, dropping the curtain, and turning quickly to face him, "But why?" she cried. "What is there for you here in New Wellington?"

He lifted one eyebrow. "For one thing…you," he said as the word *you* rolled possessively off his tongue.

"Me?" she asked wide-eyed, totally taken aback. She searched his eyes to determine if he was joking and saw that Peter was dead serious.

"Why should you stay here for me?" she exclaimed. "There was never really anything between us. You never loved me, Peter. You only used me."

169

"My dear, Rachel, it was *you* who never loved me and used me. You were the Templetons' ward, and you thought that if you married me, they would let you move back to the farm. I was a quick solution for you. That was not an easy pill to swallow, Rachel."

Giving her a wave of his hand as she tried to protest, "Yes, I admit I wanted you to sell the farm, but I wanted to take you with me to the city. I told you that."

"You know I detest city life. Always have and always will," she argued hotly.

"I was your husband," Peter reminded her. "It was your duty to go with me. And as far as I'm concerned, you still belong to me."

"It's very confusing to me, Peter, this way you're talking," she said, rubbing her hand across her forehead.

"Why should it be? It seems fairly straightforward to me."

"You twist things around. We're divorced now. And what we had is over as far as I'm concerned."

"What about Sam?" he asked, changing his tack of conversation.

"Sam?" she echoed, wide-eyed again.

"Yes. Sam Spencer," he answered as a nerve jerked in his jaw. "You two seem to be quite close. Too close, it appears to me."

"Sam is the executor of Ransom's will," she explained. "He has power over my finances."

Throwing back his head, he laughed. "Always getting yourself into that kind of situation, aren't you, Rachel? When are you going to have the say over your own money?"

She grimaced. Peter had hit a sore spot. It was just like him to be so mean.

"When I turn twenty-five," Rachel admitted fretfully as she twisted her gloved hands.

"Hmm," he said thoughtfully. Sitting down on the edge of the bed, he informed her, "Well, I might as well let you know here and now, I've bought a claim on the outside of town. Pretty good piece of property…if I do say so, myself. There are mineral springs on the land and I'm tossing some ideas around in my head for development. What I'm planning to do will rival anything they have in Lexington and more. I'm getting ready to build, and I plan to make a lot of money."

He looked at her with a vicious smile. "Just think, Rachel, you could have had me and all my money that I plan to make."

His voice jarred in her ears as his teeth gleamed in that mocking smile she knew so well.

"So you're telling me that you have no plans to leave, then?" she asked.

Peter knocked the ashes off his cigar. Drawing a puff and eyeing her through the cloud of smoke, he exhaled and said, "I thought I made that quite clear." Enjoyment at her discomfort was plain on his face.

"Yes, my dear. I am staying."

CHAPTER TWENTY-FOUR

HAYDEN AND RACHEL WALKED OUT OF THE INN, preparing to cross the street, when Sam came rushing down the walk.

"Where have you two been? You slipped out without saying good-bye," he asked, annoyance on his face and in his voice. Glancing at the inn, he jerked his head in that direction. "You've been in there, I suppose. What were you two doing at the inn?"

Rachel looked guiltily at Hayden as Hayden's face flushed red.

"Rachel wanted to talk to Brogade," Hayden explained. "So I brought her here."

"You—!" Sam sputtered. "What kind of a fool are you, bringing her to a man like that scoundrel Peter Brogade?"

Hayden threw up his hands, and Sam yelled, "If you weren't my cousin, I'd wring your neck." Poised to attack, he uttered, "Come to think of it, that's not a bad idea."

Hayden stiffened. "Now see here, Sam," he said as he took a step back. "I admit I made a mistake. Calm down and don't lose your head."

"I'll lose more than that if you ever pull a stunt like that again!" There was barely suppressed savagery in his voice.

Turning to Rachel, Sam narrowed his eyes and said, "Don't ever run off like that again."

Her embarrassment turned swiftly to anger. "Do you have to know every move I make?" Rachel questioned huffily.

"I do when you're acting strangely," Sam informed her.

She was leaving. It was one thing to speak to her like that in private, but quite another in front of people milling around the street. She was grown up. And high time he realized it.

As Rachel started to walk by him, Sam put his hands on her arms. "Where do you think you're going?"

"I'm going home, if you must know," she told him as she tried to break free.

"I'll take you," Sam stated.

"Stop treating me like a child!" she protested as she struggled against his hold. "I'm a woman and you don't seem to realize that," she said.

"Then stop acting like a child. And for your information, I treat you no differently than any other woman."

"Oh, no? What about Claudia?" she asked. "You don't tell *her* what to do and you act like the sun rises and sets on her!"

Sam's eyebrows rose, a knowing look gleamed in his eyes, and a little smile touched the corners of his mouth. "Jealous, are you?" he asked.

She was brought up short by that.

Am I? were the words that flitted through her mind.

"Don't be ridiculous!" she denied as she jerked away from him and turned to leave.

"Whatever possessed you to go to a man like Peter Brogade?" Sam asked on the ride home. "Especially the way he's treated you in the past."

"I just thought," Rachel explained, "if Peter would listen to anyone, it would be me."

"You don't understand men, Rachel. Brogade won't listen to anyone, *especially* you."

"Why do you say *especially* me?"

"Look at his past behavior. He has no morals, no scruples, and he doesn't hesitate to use anyone if he can get away with it. You're his ex-wife. A man like Brogade feels that he's entitled to privileges, though he's no longer married to you."

So that's what Peter meant by 'I still belong to him'. Ridiculous that he should think such a thing! We're divorced and that's that! Still...if Peter feels that way, he could prove to be quite a difficult enemy.

Preoccupied, she said, "Peter said something to that effect."

"What?"

"He said," Rachel responded, "'that I still belong to him'."

"I thought so," Sam nodded. "I knew by the way he looked at you." Sam covered her gloved hand with his and advised, "Rachel, Peter Brogade is dangerous to be around." After a few moments, he withdrew his hand and took back the reins.

"I don't want you to have any more dealings with him," Sam insisted. Whether she would take his advice was another thing entirely.

"Or Hayden!" he ejaculated in a fit of fury.

"Don't be too hard on Hayden," she upbraided softly. "It's entirely my fault. I convinced him to take me there."

"He should be run out of town."

"Please, Sam. It's over and done with now," she said with a trace of weariness in her voice.

Going to Peter had turned out to be a waste of time. How had she ever thought he would listen to her and just what did she think she could achieve?

Wracking her brain, she thought, "There must be some way to get through to him. Oh! Of all places for him to turn up! Why Stone Valley...and why now?"

It seemed her past would not stay behind her, but followed her at every turn. She didn't know what she would do now that Peter was taking up permanent residency.

Melancholy settled over her. She had no privacy any more. There were people around when she was in New Wellington and though she was always eager to get home, people around at North Star, as well. She needed to get away. Somewhere! Anywhere! But, with a sigh, she realized, Sam wouldn't let her go. And if he did, he would insist on going, too. All because of his promise to Ransom!

Sam was quiet for a long time. During the lapse of conversation, Rachel focused on removing her gloves. She didn't like wearing them, but Elizabeth had given her, once again, one of her little talks on the etiquette of ladies' apparel, and rather than create a rift between them, she wore them to please her...on Sunday, anyway. Laying them on her lap and ignoring another of Elizabeth's rules, she leaned her back into the seat and concentrated on the darkening skies in the East that threatened rain.

"Why didn't you ask *me* to go with you?" Sam finally asked her.

"You?" Rachel questioned, brows raised, as she turned to look at him. His strong jaw, that she always secretly admired, was set.

"You wouldn't have gone and you wouldn't have let me go, either," she pointedly said.

"You're right on both counts," he admitted. "I wouldn't have."

Turning around again to the road in front of her, "I knew that," Rachel said.

Sam grew quiet again.

"Why did you convince Hayden to go with you in the first place?" Sam finally asked.

Rachel gave a small shrug. "I needed someone waiting outside the door in case things got out of hand. I thought I could persuade Peter to leave town."

"Did you?"

"No," she answered reluctantly. "And—"

"And?"

"He's bought a claim outside of town," she told him, "and getting ready to build."

"One thing about it," Sam uttered bitterly, "Peter Brogade will get no lumber from Will Templeton."

CHAPTER TWENTY-FIVE

"BUT, PAPA," ABIGAIL CRIED AGHAST. "How could you be involved with a man like Peter Brogade?"

"I met him while I was in prison, Abby. He knew people who knew some influential people and, well...as you can see," Cabot Newgate spread his hands wide, "I'm standing here before you now. I was released from prison with his help, and I promised to help him set up a gaming hall, among other things."

"Among other things?" Abigail questioned suspiciously. "What other things?"

Cabot turned away to avoid his daughter's face. "Oh...just a business venture involving some particular ladies," he said.

Ladies?

Understanding dawned on her. "Oh, you mean wenches!" she said suddenly. "Where do you think you would get doxies such as those? You'll find none of their kind around here."

"Oh, that's no problem," he casually replied, studying his fingertips. "I've already sent for some of the women at Charleston." he informed her offhandedly. "They should be arriving any day."

She was stunned. Her mind busily considered all her father had told her. A wenching house! Women with too-tight gowns and made-up faces! Gambling and drinking! Her father's way of life in Charleston and he wanted to bring it here to New Wellington! This was a Christian community and her own father was conspiring to corrupt it!

Raising her eyes to glare at his back, she realized that he had never really changed. And she feared he had no intentions of doing so.

"But you can't do that to the people of this town!" she argued. "These are good people. Do you want to fall back into the kind of life you had in Charleston?"

Cabot was indifferent to her pleas and threw up his hands. "Don't condemn me, Abby. You know that I've had money problems. That's why I ended up in prison. I'm just trying to get by. And if this is what it takes, then, do it, I will."

Though aware of Abigail's upbringing around Charleston, South Carolina's tippling and wenching houses, New Wellington's community had been kind enough to take her in and accept her as one of them.

What was going to happen now? Would they think she was involved in all of the schemes that Peter Brogade was about to implement? How could she possibly have any further dealings with her father?

Growing up in Charleston had conditioned her somewhat to accepting a licentious lifestyle as normal. Though Cabot had protected her enough to keep her from following the same road, still, she was aware of what went on. Born the daughter of an unwed madam who had died in childbirth, she was never accepted among the elite of Charleston and had ended up using her skills as a teacher for the children of the prostitutes.

But Abigail had become a different person in New Wellington. Coming on the journey and living among the inhabitants of this new town, Abigail was accepted among the godly towns-folk, which allowed her to see a completely different way of living. And she liked what she saw. She was a member of the community, schoolteacher, and a member of the New Wellington Church. She might have gone along with her father's bawdy and promiscuous lifestyle while in Charleston, but she could not do so here. Not now. Not ever again.

And now she was married to Gabe Roswell. Gabe! What would he think? He knew her past, of course, and loved her in spite of it. Would he hate her now that her father had come to undermine the principles of the town? Would she lose her job as teacher? Would she remain a member of the church? If Gabe knew her father was under their roof at this moment—well—she shuddered to think what might happen.

"Oh, Papa! Please don't ask to stay here at the house. Gabe would never permit it. He's a Christian now and would never take you in under these circumstances."

Cabot turned back to her. "You don't have to. I've got a room at the inn...paid for by Peter Brogade, as a matter of fact. As soon as the arrangements are completed, I will be staying at Brogade's."

There was no point arguing with him, she realized now. His mind was made up and he cared little that her standing in the community might be jeopardized.

"How long before you open the hall?" she finally quietly asked.

"Just a few more days."

Abigail stared at her father and for the first time in her life, she despised him. Oh, he had tried to act like a Christian at times, but, in reality, the fruit of a Christian life was not there. He had lived the life of a hypocrite, and that she could not forgive him for. Not while he continued the role he was playing.

How could he do this to her? Right by her own back door! And what if children should be born to her marriage? How could she explain their grandfather to them? She hated to admit it to herself, but better that he had remained in prison.

Rachel had confided her own fears about Peter Brogade to her. She understood now how Rachel felt. Truly, she did. And if there was any way to get rid of Brogade and her father as well, she would support it wholeheartedly. Short of murder, that is.

CHAPTER TWENTY-SIX

IT WAS SUNDAY. Hayden was pursuing Rachel openly and ardently, and Oliver decided it was time to return to Virginia, taking Hayden in tow.

"Hayden wants me to marry him," Rachel informed Sam on the way home from dinner at the parsonage.

"So," Sam said guardedly, "I suppose you want my approval for the marriage?"

"Yes. Ransom stipulated in his will that I must have it. I don't have to tell you that."

She didn't love Hayden—hadn't really been in love with any man—not like a woman should. Some instinct in Sam told him that. He knew she had a kind heart, but that was about as far as it went. Sam knew Rachel cared about Ransom and missed him, but love that animates every fiber of your being—no. She had never known that.

"You'll have to explain why you want to marry Hayden," Sam told her. "As you said, my approval is necessary."

"Yes, I know."

"So—do you want to tell me your reasons for such a marriage?"

Rachel took a deep breath. "Well...for starters, Hayden is good to me." She ran her hand over her cheek as their last encounter flitted through her mind. She had finally allowed a chaste peck.

"And he makes me laugh," she added.

"That's your criteria for marriage?" Sam asked incredulously. "Someone who makes you laugh?"

At her silence, Sam grew moody. He knew his father was leaving. Oliver had told him so. "Taking Hayden with me," he'd said. Yet, in his wildest dreams, Sam never expected Hayden to be so persuasive in charming Rachel to leave, too. The thought of losing her was making his heart beat a little too fast and his stomach feel a little sick.

"Where do you plan to live?" he asked, keeping his voice on an even tone.

Rachel put on a happy face that did not convince him. "We could live part of the time in Philadelphia and part of the time at North Star."

"You would never be happy in the political world. You would miss North Star too much."

"We would make it work," said Rachel, trying to dispel the doubt she was feeling. "I know we would."

Sam clenched his teeth. So hard, that he was in danger of chipping a tooth.

"Hayden's not a Christian. Did you even consider that?"

She had. "Yes, I've considered it. You're right about that. He's not a Christian. Not now." Rachel added brightly, "But I believe he will be someday."

"What you plan to do is not scriptural. A believer is not to marry an unbeliever. That's what the Bible says."

She had no answer to that.

"What about love?" Sam continued. "Have you even remotely thought about that?"

"Hayden says he loves me," she said slowly. "He's very devoted to me."

"And you? What about you? Do you love him?"

"I'm very fond of Hayden," she admitted truthfully.

"Fond!" Sam scoffed and rolled his eyes.

"Yes, fond," she spoke in defense. "A good marriage doesn't necessarily have to have love, as long as it is based on mutual respect," she answered loftily.

"Who thought of that line?" he gruffly said. "I know it certainly wasn't you."

"Well…as a matter-of-fact…it was Hayden. I was quite honest with him. I told him that I was fond of him, but nothing more."

"Well, thank goodness for that!"

"Hayden feels the marriage will work out fine. He thinks Mother would be pleased if she were here."

"I don't think it will work! And I don't think your mother would be pleased, either." If he thought giving her a good shaking would do any good, he would. "Knowing you'll be entering into a marriage without love, how can you agree?"

"You won't listen to what I want at all!"

"It's not what *you* really want. It's what Hayden wants. You don't love him and wouldn't be happy with him. He can't be faithful to any one woman. He's proven that in the past and he won't be to you. What do you think will happen? Divorce? Again?"

"You don't know what I want!" she exclaimed, with a little stomp of her foot. "You never agree with what I want. I'll tell you what I want. I want your approval!"

"Rachel!" Sam interrupted. He pulled the horse to a sudden stop and Rachel lurched forward and grabbed her hat. Before she could settle back in the seat, he turned to her, took her chin in his hand, and looked straight into her eyes. As he forced her to look at him, Rachel saw something in his eyes she had never seen before. She had seen him angry, but not this kind of anger, a different anger— full of force and passion.

"Wha—?" she asked, wide-eyed.

"Are you going to settle again?" he asked in a stormy voice. "You're always settling to obtain what you think you want. You settled for Peter to live on the farm. You settled for Ransom to get out of Wellington. You think marrying Hayden is an easy way out of your financial situation now. Quit putting blinders on. When you take them off and see things clearly, it's always been too late. You have a choice now. Make the right one. Settle for Hayden or—"

Sam nearly said 'marry me'. But she wasn't ready for his declaration. Not yet. Rachel had entered marriage too lightly twice before and Sam was determined it would not happen a third time. Not with him anyway. He would know when she fell completely in love with him and he could, if somewhat impatiently, bide his time.

"Or—?" Rachel began, then her voice faltered and she stopped. His eyes captivated her as they darkened from cornflower to dark blue. She gazed back mutely as heat washed over her cheeks. His eyes strayed to her lips, and she thought as he leaned in that he was going to kiss her.

Raising his eyes again, Sam looked long and hard into her own expectant ones. Then he turned, picked up the reins, snapped them, and said, "Wait for the right man. The man God has planned for you."

Rachel was let down...again. If he had tried to kiss her, she would have kissed him back. Knew it as surely as she knew that today was Sunday.

They were silent for a time. There was a longing in the pit of Sam's stomach while Rachel's thoughts buzzed around in her head.

How could I have wanted Sam to kiss me if I'm trying to convince him to allow me to marry Hayden? Hayden doesn't stir me like Sam does.

Searching her heart, Rachel knew, beyond a doubt, that she'd rather be with Sam today than anyone else. Rachel stole a look at him. She might be unsophisticated, but the look in his eyes was a look any woman could read. He baffled her. Did he want her for himself? He never said he loved her, yet he wanted to keep her from marrying Hayden. What was he waiting for?

Quietly, she asked, "How do you know that Hayden is not the right man for me?"

His heart was thundering in his chest and he didn't trust himself to speak.

"Sam?" she asked.

Finally, he said, "I just listed the reasons. For once in your life don't be hardheaded." he chided her, but softened his tone.

"So…you're telling me no?" she asked.

Almost inaudibly. he answered, "You know the answer to that question."

"I want to hear it from your own lips," she baited him. "What is your answer?"

Sam knew he would be even further down on her blacklist should he answer. Winning points with her was not easy. But easy was not always right—especially in her case.

Looking straight ahead, he answered softly, "No. You cannot marry Hayden."

CHAPTER TWENTY-SEVEN

THE HALL OPENED AND THE WENCHES ARRIVED just as Cabot Newgate predicted they would. Peter's connections in Logan County soon frequented the hall even as he was making plans to expand his holdings to draw the upper echelons of Lexington's society.

Several weeks had passed with no further word from Peter. Then, as Rachel was poring over the accounts at Templeton Store, a rap was heard on the office door.

Thinking it was the boy working in the front, she called to the closed door, "Come in, Emmett."

The door opened slowly and in walked a man she'd never seen before...young and tall, with black hair, and a tiny scar above one eyebrow.

"Mrs. Templeton?" The stranger spoke in a voice oddly pleasant to the ear. The flat, slow drawl of a Charlestonian, immediately reminiscent of Peter and Cabot Newgate.

"Yes, I'm Mrs. Templeton."

"My name's Race Holloway, ma'am," he said, removing his hat.

"Yes, Mr. Holloway. May I help you?"

"Uh...more like, I have a message for you."

"A message for me?" she questioned, "From whom?"

He shrugged and leaned across the desk, holding out a folded paper to her. "I think you need to read this for yourself."

Drawing her brows together, she looked at the note for a few seconds. Then cautiously, took it from Mr. Holloway's hand. "What's this all about?" she asked.

"Like I said, you need to read it for yourself."

"Well...yes, thank you, Mr. Holloway for delivering it to me."

Race stood still.

With a questioning look on her face, Rachel asked, "Is there anything else, Mr. Holloway?"

"I was told to wait for your reply."

"All right. Please have a seat."

Still, he stood.

Eyeing him suspiciously, Rachel leaned back in the chair and proceeded to unfold the note.

As she read, her eyes grew wide and a moan escaped her lips. "No! It can't be!" she uttered in horror.

Turning terrified eyes upon Holloway, she asked in a whisper, "What does this mean? What does Peter want with me?"

Race's eyes gleamed oddly, "Like the note says, Mrs. Templeton. Meet him there at five o'clock. He'll tell you himself."

Holloway turned to walk out the door. Looking back one last time, he warned, "If I were you, Mrs. Templeton, I'd do like he says. If you don't want anyone to get hurt, that is."

Her heart turned to stone and she mumbled through lips that had gone numb. "Tell Peter I'll be there."

Dazed, Rachel had forgotten all but Peter's note, when a knock at the door sounded. How long had she been sitting there like that?

"Mrs. Templeton?" sounded Emmett's voice on the other side of the door

"Mrs. Templeton?" came the voice again.

The knob turned and Emmett warily opened the door, not knowing what to expect.

Peeking around the door, he asked, "Mrs. Templeton? Are you all right? Is there any trouble?"

Looking up at his pimply, juvenile face, with a wave of her hand, she answered, "Yes, Emmett, I'm fine."

Rachel looked strange...different than he had ever seen her. There was a weird wildness about her eyes and he tentatively offered, "Ma'am. It's half past four...time for me to leave. Do you need me for anything else today?"

"Wha—what did you say?"

"I said, ma'am, it's four-thirty. Can I go home now?"

Half past four! She thought, coming out of her daze. She had to be at Peter's place at five! She would have to lock the store, go to the livery and rent a horse. Could she make it in time? She had to!

"Yes," she answered. "Yes, of course, Emmett. You can leave."

"All right, ma'am. See you tomorrow, then."

Glancing past him as though she saw the ghosts of her past, she answered automatically, "Of course...of course. See you tomorrow."

Rachel pulled back on the reins and steered her horse toward the side of the building. She was stunned to see so many horses tethered so early in the evening.

Nearly colliding with an impromptu horse race that was underway, she had a fleeting glimpse of Race Holloway's face as he rounded the building, black hair rushing in the wind, a look of pure pleasure on his face as he spurred on his black stallion.

Taken by surprise at the sight of her, his attention wavered—but only for a moment. Then, he was engrossed in the race once again.

When the dust settled, she snapped the reins and approached the back of the building as Peter had instructed in the note.

Collecting her thoughts, she didn't want to go in, and actually considered turning and leaving. But Peter had written that if she did not come, someone's life would be in danger. What could he possibly mean? Who was he talking about?

An elderly man, gray-haired and bent with age, someone she had never seen before, walked out of the shadows and reaching her horse, held him by the bridle. As she prepared to dismount, he moved to help her. She doubted from the looks of him if he had the strength to help anyone, but she acted as though he were the strongest of men and allowed him to lift her down.

"Thank you," she said.

Nodding to her, the man merely grunted and busied himself tying the horse to the rail.

It was a two-story building with a door opening to the back on each floor. The area around the ground-level door was littered with empty whiskey casks and bottles.

Glancing up, she wondered if Peter's office could be located on the second floor. He never specified in the note which door. Undecided, she turned to the little man who was already disappearing into the shadows and asked where Peter Brogade's office was located.

He merely jerked his thumb toward the top of the stairs as he threw another grunt over his shoulder.

Gathering her skirts about her, she climbed the stairs and crossing to the door, gave a tentative knock.

A few seconds later the door opened and Peter stood there with a scowl on his face.

"You're late," he accused as he motioned her into the room while glancing at his pocket watch.

"I had to go to the livery and rent a horse after I got off work," she explained. She stepped into the room and Peter snapped the watch shut and closed the door.

Looking around the room that was obviously Peter's office, Rachel had to admit it was finer than anything she had seen in New Wellington, including Will and Jane's new home. Whatever bad she had to say about Peter, it was not that he lacked good taste in furnishings. She supposed that in all his travels, he had picked up a sense of taste and appetite for opulence.

Rachel turned to him expectantly. Peter looked her over slowly, thoroughly enjoying what he saw. He laughed and moved closer to her. She had the sudden urge to slap his face. No one dared to look at her like that and his impudence offended her.

"Well, I'm here," she said, trying unsuccessfully to keep the anger out of her voice.

"Yes," he smiled, "I see."

"What did you want to see me about, Peter?" she asked, coming right to the point.

He waved his hand at her. "All in good time."

Peter motioned for her to sit in one of the plush chairs and, rather than cause a fuss, she did as he indicated. Walking to the massive sideboard, he asked, "Would you care for a drink?" Looking over his shoulder, he saw her head shaking no.

"No, of course not—nothing stronger than tea—I remember." Pouring his own drink, he said, "That can be arranged."

Rachel started to protest, but Peter strode to the back door, opened it and called, "Jeremiah!"

She cringed at his tone.

Within thirty seconds, the old man, who had assisted her, appeared.

"Remarkable," Rachel thought, "that a man of his age can move so fast."

Jeremiah waited quietly inside the door while Peter instructed, "Get Mrs. Templeton some tea—now!"

Rachel cringed again.

Jeremiah moved across the room, his feet shuffling along on the carpet, and disappeared through the office door.

"Shut the door!" Peter yelled, and Jeremiah instantly reappeared and pulled the door shut.

Turning to look at Rachel's disapproving face, Peter walked to the front of the disorderly desk and pushing some papers to one side, sat on the edge, one leg dangling while he cupped the glass in his hands.

After making small talk about his future plans for Brogade Palace, Peter came to the heart of his threatening request.

"As to the reason I wanted to see you, Rachel...I need some help in the office. You can see by this mess on my desk that I really need someone to keep accounts. And I know you have some experience in that area, working at Templeton Store."

CHAPTER TWENTY-EIGHT

RACHEL STARED AT PETER IN DISBELIEF.

"You want me to keep your books? Here?"

Never in her wildest dreams had she suspected that Peter would ask her to work in this gutter of society.

"I don't believe it!" she sputtered.

Peter smiled an enchanting smile at her. "Why should that be so hard to believe? After all, you're my wife. And a wife is supposed to help her husband."

"Ex-wife!" she nearly shouted. "Can't you get that through your head? Ex-wife! You and I are divorced, Peter. It's over."

Rachel started to get up and he quickly rose and pushed her back into the chair with one hand.

"Is it, my sweet?" he asked.

"Yes! It is! Of all the impudent—"

The door opened without warning and Jeremiah shuffled through it, carrying a cup of tea. Rachel snapped her mouth shut while she fumed. Jeremiah stopped inside the door and stood there.

"Give it to her, you idiot!" Peter ordered. Again, Rachel recoiled at the tone of Peter's voice.

Jeremiah shuffled to Rachel and handed her the tea. She felt sorry for him. Glancing into his weathered face, Rachel gave a little smile and softly said, "Thank you, Jeremiah."

Rachel thought she noticed the faintest of smiles touch the corners of his mouth.

Jeremiah waited.

"You can go," Peter said. Jerking his head toward the back door, he barked, "Go out and keep an eye on things."

Looking at Rachel meaningfully, "If anyone unexpected comes, let me know," he added.

Jeremiah, in his same old shuffle, crossed the room, opened the door, and glancing back momentarily at Rachel, closed it behind him, disappearing as silently as he had come.

"As I was saying," Peter continued, as he sat back on the desk, "I need someone to keep my ledgers. I can't depend on the girls here. They're only interested in turning their—well, they have other things on their mind. And I can't trust my partners. They would rob me blind."

Looking her up and down, he said, "I know I can trust you. Yes, I think you will fill the bill quite nicely."

His face softened momentarily, and he said, "There's nothing like having a pretty face around...especially one that belongs to me."

Rachel stared at him. She must be having a bad dream.

When she didn't answer, he raised the glass to his mouth. Watching him bolt the whiskey, it was apparent that he was not going to take no for an answer, and she wondered what he knew about her that would get her to agree to his bizarre proposal.

"What makes you think that I would submit to this—this outlandish scheme of yours?" she sarcastically asked.

"Oh, I think you will," he answered confidently.

"Why? Pray tell."

"Because, Rachel, I've obtained a bit of information that will persuade you."

"What bit of information?"

"Your son."

Rachel was stunned. "My son? Payne?"

"Yes. Why didn't you tell me you had a son?"

That's what he meant in the note by 'someone could get hurt'.

"Why should I want you, of all people, to know I have a child?" she asked.

Ignoring her question, Peter said, "I suppose it's Ransom's."

"Yes! Of course, he's Ransom's child!"

Shaking with anger, she jumped to her feet, dropping her cup, and he didn't stop her this time. "I'm warning you, Peter! You leave my child alone!"

She turned to walk away from him, but rising, he grabbed her arm and swung her around.

"You're warning me?" he asked dangerously.

"Yes! I'll kill you if you so much as touch a hair on Payne's head!" she threatened.

He laughed and dropped his hand. "You have a lot of spirit, Rachel. More so now than I ever saw in Wellington. You wouldn't have dared to talk to me like that before."

"This is *New* Wellington!" she cried. "And Payne is my son. You leave him alone, Peter!"

Hedging, Peter drawled, "Oh...I'll leave him alone, if...."

"If what?" she asked uneasily.

"If you do what I say," Peter said in a deadly, quiet voice.

"You beast!" Rachel exclaimed. How dare he threaten her baby! Feeling a strong urge to scratch his eyes out, she restrained herself by balling her fists into knots.

"What if he was your child, Peter? How would you feel if someone threatened him?"

"I don't have any children," he shrugged, "so it makes little difference to me."

"But you did!" Rachel blurted.

He was stunned. He thought back to the two months they had spent together as man and wife. His eyes narrowed and he grabbed her wrist, tightening his fingers around it.

She cried out in pain.

"What do you mean, I did?" He squeezed and shook her wrist so hard she thought it would break.

Trying to pull away, Rachel writhed desperately. "Yes, you... we did," she gasped. "The child was a girl."

"A daughter?" he asked as he stared wide-eyed at Rachel. "I have a daughter?"

Rachel had not meant to mention it to him, but he riled her so.

"Where is she?" he demanded, a threatening look on his face as he threw the empty glass he was holding in the other hand across the room. The glass hit the stone fireplace and shattered into a hundred pieces. "Tell me or...."

"She's dead," Rachel uttered triumphantly, eyes blazing with revenge.

Peter blinked hard and gave her a considering look. "How?" he asked as his hand loosened and slipped from her wrist.

"Stillborn," Rachel answered as she straightened. Watching Peter's face, the triumph slowly slipped from her, and a passionate sadness rose within her as she thought of that spring morning not so long ago when Ransom delivered Peter's lifeless baby.

With her shoulders slumping, and her hand massaging the wrist that would surely boast some bruises in the morning, she said again softly, "Our child was stillborn."

Peter reeled at this bit of news and fell back against the desk. He looked at Rachel and knew it was true. The pain of a woman who had lost her child was unmistakable on her face.

"Why didn't you contact me when you found out that you were pregnant?" Peter asked in a more subdued tone. "I would have come back to Wellington straightaway."

"And just how was I supposed to know where to contact you?" she bitterly accused. "You left town and I didn't know where you were until I got the divorce papers stating you were in Prince William County."

He sighed. Rising and walking around the desk, Peter slumped heavily into the chair. "There's nothing I can do about that now," he said more into the air than to her.

After a few moments, he looked at her again, "But I will say, that we have a closer tie than I previously realized, knowing that you carried my child."

Rachel now realized that this bit of information she'd let slip had only reinforced Peter's inordinate attachment to her.

The anger gone, she quietly pleaded, "Please. I'm asking you, Peter. Please don't harm my son."

He had her. She would do his bidding. He knew it.

His voice was casual when he sounded the death knell of her reputation.

"I won't...if you'll come and work for me," he stipulated. "Just be grateful that I'm not asking for more."

Rachel arrived at the livery to return the rented horse. "Put it on my account," she told Art Jenkins. "Sam will pay the bill."

Walking through town, wondering how she would get home, Rachel heard her name called. Turning, she saw Sam draw the buggy up beside the walk.

196

"Get in," Sam called as he got out. "Where in the world have you been?" he asked tersely. "I've been looking everywhere for you."

It had become routine for Sam to pick Rachel up in the morning and bring her to town and take her home at night. She was exhausted right now, as any run-in with Peter always left her feeling that way. Climbing into the buggy after her, Sam noticed that her face was drawn.

"Well?" he asked as he took the reins.

"Please," Rachel pleaded, "just drive me home."

Peter's place and his demands were still too fresh in her mind. She had to do what he wanted. What else could she do? And what would people—never mind, she knew what people would say. But she had Payne to protect, above all else. If she didn't go along with Peter's demands, he would carry out his threats. She knew he would. Suddenly she felt old—old beyond her years.

Sam snapped the reins, turned the horse in the middle of the street, and headed toward North Star.

When they were on the main road, he asked, "Are you going to tell me?"

She wearily shook her head no. "I'll say this much," she ventured. "I'll be taking myself to town and home at night."

"You're not going to tell me?"

"Not yet. I'm just not up to it right now, Sam."

Rachel arrived home from the Palace. She had been working for two days setting up the ledgers for Peter. In addition to receipts and expenditures, she had been told that part of her duties was to keep track of all inventories.

Frank and the men were putting the finishing touches on her new home and as she opened the door and walked across the threshold, she spotted Payne crawling on the floor with Louise following behind him.

"Payne! My baby!" Rachel cried as she rushed to pick him up. Cradling him as tightly as she could, she looked over the top of his head and met Louise's troubled eyes. Drawing her brows into a frown, Rachel asked, "Is something wrong, Louise? Has something happened?"

"Let's go into the parlor, Rachel. There's something I need to discuss with you."

A feeling of doom descended over Rachel. Had someone from the Palace been here?

Settling onto the settee, Rachel asked, "What is it, Louise?"

Louise looked uncomfortable as she said, "There's something I need to tell you, Rachel."

"Yes?" Rachel looked puzzled. "Go on."

"It's like this," Louise began, not meeting Rachel's eyes, "Frank has bought a claim not too far from here and we're thinking about settling on it. It might be best if you look for someone else to run the place," she said distantly.

"I can understand why you want your own place, Louise. But would you tell me, is there something I've done that has offended you?"

Louise folded her hands in her lap as her lips pursed. "There's no sense in beating about the bush, Rachel. Frank has heard some gossip in town. Folks say you're not working at Templeton Store anymore. They say you're working at that gambling place outside of town."

"Yes, that's true," Rachel admitted.

"Not meaning to hurt your feelings, Rachel, as you have been mighty good to us, but we just can't have any part in such goings-on. Frank and I have talked this all out. I'm sure you understand. Frankly, we're disappointed in you."

Rachel had expected as much. A person couldn't keep something like this a secret for very long. Rachel had noticed Frank avoiding her yesterday evening. But, being the gentleman he was, he kept his opinions to himself.

"Could you possibly stay until I find someone to replace you?" Rachel asked.

"I'll talk to Frank about it, but we'd like to move on as quickly as possible."

"Yes, of course. I understand."

She would talk about the matter to Sam in the morning, Rachel told her, hoping that Sam had not heard the news yet.

CHAPTER TWENTY-NINE

SAM HAD. When Rachel walked into his office the next morning, he exploded.

"What the—what in the world prompted you to quit Templeton Store and work for that black-hearted, no-good, ex-husband of yours? Haven't you had enough trouble with him in the past?"

Rachel kept her eyes riveted to the floor.

"It was bad enough that he brought his gambling and prostitution here, but to find that you have gone over to his side...are you insane?" His voice had raised another notch.

At that moment she wished she hadn't come, but it made no difference. He would have sought her out, demanding an explanation.

"I can't tell you why."

Frustrated, he blew out a breath. "Why not?" Sam asked in exasperation.

"I just can't. You tend to your business and I'll tend to mine."

"Your business *is* my business."

Sam ran his hand through his hair, clearly agitated. "Honestly, Rachel, I can't figure you out. Some of the crazy stunts you pull sometimes."

Sam paced the floor behind her. "You would not do this willingly. There must be some reason why you're over there, but for the life of me, I don't know what it is. Would you care to enlighten me?"

Rachel shook her head no.

Sam walked behind his desk and stared at her. "Look at me," he said.

She looked up and he saw tears in her eyes, threatening to spill over. "Something's wrong. I know it."

"Louise and Frank are quitting me, Sam. That's why I'm here. I need another overseer at my place."

Sam's sixth sense as an attorney kicked in. He searched her face. "No. That's not it. There's something else wrong."

Rachel watched as Sam put his hands on his hips and turned away from her in intense thought.

He tried to come to some logical conclusion, but there wasn't any. She detested such places as Brogade Palace. Caring so much what other people thought about her, he knew she would not voluntarily work at the hall. Why? And with her ex-husband, to boot.

He turned back again. Examining her eyes, he saw fear in them and recognition dawned on his face. He snapped his fingers. "I know what it is. You're afraid. And it has to do with your ex-husband."

He narrowed his eyes. "What does Brogade have hanging over your head?"

Terror leaped into her eyes and she answered in a frantic whisper. "Please, Sam. I can't tell you."

"Why not?"

"Because." Throwing her hands up at him, she said, "Just—just, don't ask me any more questions, Sam."

At his look, the one she had come to know so well, Rachel knew it was just a matter of time before Sam extracted the information from her. After debating it for a few seconds she decided it was better to say something now than go through his experienced, grueling interrogation. He wouldn't give up until she confessed. She was simply not up to that this morning.

"Someone's life is in danger," Rachel said reluctantly. "That's why I'm working there." Picturing Payne's little face in her mind, her heart contracted at the memory. His smile, when she walked into the door at night, gurgling at her with delight.

Maybe Sam would leave it at this. But her hopes were dashed at his next question.

"Whose?"

She dropped her head while shaking it again.

Something was terribly wrong. Sam could read the panic on Rachel's face. When she didn't answer, Sam stepped out from behind the desk, crossed to her in two strides, and grasped her wrist. She winced involuntarily, cried out, and bit her lip.

He let go immediately. "What's wrong with your arm?" he asked.

"It doesn't matter," she said.

"It does to me. Let me see."

She backed away from him but he grabbed her elbow. Pushing up her sleeve, Sam saw the massive bruising shining purple on her wrist.

"Did Brogade do this?" Sam questioned impatiently, his blood pressure rising. Inside, he was exploding and he was tempted to get a gun and shoot Peter Brogade at that wretched palace of his. But the attorney side of him said to wait and investigate the situation before running off and getting engaged in a gun-fight.

Rachel kept silent.

"I see. He did." Pulling her sleeve back down, "I'll take you to Doctor Stone," he said, and moved away from her.

Asking in a calmer voice, "Tell me then, whose life is in danger? Yours?"

Rachel shook her head.

Sam wrinkled his forehead trying to figure out who it could be.

"There's no one you would be so worried about unless…."

His eyes widened. "Payne? Your son?"

Rachel's lower lip began to tremble and she lapsed into tears and then he knew. It *was* Payne. Peter had threatened her son. Sam reached for her and she fell into his arms. She balled up a fist and half-heartedly hit him on the chest while venting frustrated sobs.

"Shh," Sam murmured against her hair. "There, there. It will be all right."

"Oh, Sam! I'm so frightened!" Rachel cried in real distress. "Peter is blackmailing me into working at the palace. He says he'll do something to Payne if I don't do what he says!" she cried desperately, her courage and control breaking. "He's just crazy enough to do it!"

"Don't cry. It'll be all right. I'll think of something," Sam said soothingly. "I guess the best thing to do is to haul him into court. This is against the law."

"Oh, no!" she cried, raising her face to his. "No one is supposed to know. Peter will kidnap Payne and do something to him if he finds out that I told you. I know him. He won't stop at anything."

Pulling desperately on Sam's shirt, bringing his face closer to hers, she pleaded, "Don't, Sam. Don't tell anyone. It will just be my word against Peter's and you know no court will find him guilty without any evidence."

Sam looked at her desperate, tear-streaked face. "But Rachel," he reasoned, "it's probably the best chance you have, if we get him now. We'll take Payne to safety somewhere and then take Peter to court."

Rachel backed up from him. "No!" she cried indignantly, spittle thick in her mouth. "Peter will find him," she said in a rush. "You don't know him like I do. He'll stop at nothing to get his way." She leaned into Sam again, clutching his shirt. "Please, Sam. Do this my way. I'll think of something. I'll go out of my mind if I think there's any danger to Payne."

Looking into her eyes, Sam softened. This was, after all, her son. If it were his child, he would undoubtedly feel the same way.

Finally: "What do you suggest that we do, then?"

Rachel released Sam and turned to pace the floor. Finally, she said decidedly, "I'll keep working there for a while. Let me find out what I can about his business dealings. With Cabot Newgate involved, there must be plenty of underhanded shenanigans going on. If we can convict him that way, then so be it. Just as long as he doesn't suspect that anyone knows about Payne."

Stopping in front of Sam, she commented, "Peter is evil, but he's still a little stupid when it comes to me."

Sam didn't like it, but there didn't seem to be any alternative. Rachel was putting herself in danger and he wouldn't be there to protect her.

"You realize that if you play detective, the town will turn against you, if they haven't already? News travels fast, you know. You'll be an outcast to the folk of New Wellington."

"So, do you think this will be the first time that I've been an outcast?" Rachel asked with a brittle laugh.

CHAPTER THIRTY

AS SAM HAD PREDICTED, the news traveled fast. It was the talk of every household in New Wellington. Some of the residents had been scandalized by Rachel's past behavior, but in time they had come to overlook her actions, blaming it on her immaturity. And it didn't hurt any that she had been the ward of the beloved Pastor and Mrs. Templeton. But all the previous criticism of her earlier escapades was nothing compared to the gossip that buzzed throughout the town now.

Rachel didn't show her face at Sunday meeting and the Templeton household was in a tizzy.

"Imagine," Jane interjected in the flurry of words exchanged, "Rachel working at that bawdy house outside of town. I think it might be a good idea if you took her to court, Jacob, and gained custody of Payne. It doesn't seem that she is a fit mother and Payne is your grandson, after all."

Jacob threw her a look that defied any further disparaging of Rachel's character. "I don't think that's a good idea, Jane. Rachel must have some reason to be working at that place. Let's give her a while longer until we find out what's going on."

"Ransom would be turning over in his grave if he knew what Rachel was doing," Will said. He was hurt. He liked Rachel, but her latest episode had him bewildered. It was enough that he was trying to come to terms with the fact that she had abruptly left her work at the store and taken up with Brogade, but to listen to others talk about it all day at the mill grated on his nerves. He half-threatened to throw everyone off of the place.

"Talk is—that she's doing the same things as those bawdy girls in there," Jane said with an upturned nose.

"Jane!" James said. "You know Rachel better than that."

"James, we all know that she's been in a snit over her money. Who knows what goes on?"

"That's enough of that, Jane," Will warned.

Cissa kept quiet through the whole conversation. She knew Rachel better than the rest. If she could just get to her and find out what was going through her head, maybe she could help.

Ignoring Will's warning, Jane said, "It's just scandalous…simply scandalous."

John Winslow arrived from Virginia with a party. He had been in New Wellington about ten minutes when he heard the news. Upon hearing the gossip, he deposited the party at the parsonage and made a beeline to Rachel's house.

"Pa!" Rachel cried when he walked through the door. "When did you get back?"

He threw his hands up at her and gave her a stern look. "Never mind when I got back. Do you want to tell me, young lady, what possessed you to start working at Brogade's? I know your finances have had you upset, but is money that important to you?"

Rachel tried to choke back the lump that formed in her throat. Her father looked so angry and sounded much harsher than he had ever sounded.

"I can't tell you that, Pa," she said evasively.

"Can't tell me? And just why not? Never has anyone in our family shown such flagrant behavior such as yours. I've got a great mind to leave here and take Payne with me."

"Don't do that, Pa," she pleaded. "Please. Just talk to Sam. He'll straighten everything out."

"He'd better," John warned.

Dropping by Sam's that evening, it seemed an eternity to John before Sam came in with the herd. Spying Sam in the distance, John stepped up on his horse and galloped across the pasture. Pulling up beside a surprised Sam, John snapped, "Rachel said you would explain what's going on. I'm warning you, you'd better not be in this with her. I'll give you about three seconds to start telling me."

Holding up his hand to ward John off, Sam signaled to his foreman. "Cantrell, take the herd in."

"Right, boss," Cantrell called back.

Turning to John, Sam said, "Come back to the cabin, John. And I'll explain."

Once inside, John exploded once again. "Out with it, Sam! I want to know what's going on with Rachel."

"Now, John," Sam said in a calm voice. "It's not what you think. Rachel's in a real predicament. If I have your word that you'll keep mum about this, I'll tell you."

It was hard to calm down, but John forced himself. "Go ahead."

"Promise?"

"Yes," he answered, though he was struggling.

"It seems Brogade has threatened to do something to Payne if Rachel doesn't cooperate with him at that palace."

John exploded again. "How dare that—! I'll get a gun and kill the sorry cuss."

"Don't do that, John. If you do, then we'll be hauling you into court. Then, what would Rachel and Payne do?"

John didn't like it. Didn't like what Brogade was doing to his daughter and her reputation.

"I know what you've heard, that's she's prostituting herself," Sam continued, "but that simply isn't so. She's keeping his books. I wanted to take him to court, but Rachel felt it would be better to work undercover to bring down his shady dealings. As much as I was against her putting herself in danger, it seems that might be the best way. You can understand her concern for her son."

He could, but that didn't mean he liked it any better.

"The law hasn't caught up with Brogade so far," John said, irate. "What makes you think Rachel can find out anything?"

"We don't know what kind of trouble he's been in. There's one thing I do believe...he'll slip up somewhere," Sam assured. "His kind always does. Then we'll lock him up for a long, long time."

"Maybe."

"I believe it would work if Rachel relays any information she finds out to us and we worked on the legalities on this end."

John was worried. His only child working in a place like that, putting herself in harm's way, and he as much as told Sam that.

"I understand," Sam agreed. "But the more I thought about it, if Rachel can bring down his house of ill repute, it will keep his operations from spreading in this community and maybe in the state. There's talk that he's got connections in Lexington. I suspect it's through Cabot Newgate."

"Yeah. I know Newgate and his past. Between his tippling houses and houses of prostitution, he's been a pretty low-life character. If he so much as touches one hair on her head—!"

"Calm down, John."

John chewed the inside of his cheek as his mind whirled. "You know what a temper Rachel has, Sam. She'll mess up and get herself in trouble."

"I know she does," Sam nodded in agreement. "But she's thinking about Payne right now. And as long as Payne's safety is her objective, she'll keep her head about her."

John felt utterly at a loss. His only child. The pride and joy of his life and he was expected to sit idly by. "What do you want me to do?"

"Well, for starters, I think it might be a good idea if you travel up to Lexington and nose around for a while. Pose as a...let's see—" he said as he rubbed his forehead, "Yes I've got it! You can say you're a horse buyer. That way, some doors might open that wouldn't ordinarily. I hear a young man that works at Brogade's by the name of Race Holloway, is a big fan of horses. There's talk about his father living in Lexington. See what you can find out about his name and look him up. Could be this is the link we are looking for."

"When do you want me to leave?"

"As soon as possible. Come to my office tomorrow and we'll try to formulate a plan. I'll see about getting you some money to throw around in Lexington."

"When I do this," John asked, "should I keep my own name?"

"Probably. If anyone gets suspicious, they'll check to see if you're on the up and up."

"Brogade would remember that Rachel's maiden name is Winslow. Think he would connect us together?"

"You've never met him?"

"No. I was in Kentucky when she met and married him. She was already divorced by the time I got back to Virginia."

"Hmm…that could be a problem."

"I guess there's not much we can do about that. If it's mentioned, I'll just pass it off as some coincidence."

"By the way, John, buy a decent suit of clothes…just for impression's sake."

Sam convinced Frank and Louise to stay on a while, citing the difficulty in finding suitable help to manage North Star. John left for Lexington and Sam kept in close contact with Rachel. Rachel switched her working hours to the afternoon and early evening so that she might observe anything suspicious.

When questioned by Peter as to why she wanted to do so, she answered that it was difficult to do her job if he was sleeping most of the day away and wasn't there to answer any questions she might have. That sounded plausible to him and he thought nothing more about it.

In fact, his vanity was touched. Peter thought she wanted to be near him.

CHAPTER THIRTY-ONE

"I'M GLAD RACHEL TURNED ME DOWN," Hayden remarked as he, Oliver, and Sam breakfasted at the café. "Looks like I wasn't a very good judge of character. Did she ever have me fooled!"

Sam tightened his grip on the edge of the table. He was glad things were finally over between Hayden and Rachel, but it burned on the tip of his tongue to spit out words in her defense.

Instead, "Just be glad you're getting out now," Sam said. Turning to Oliver, "You're leaving in the morning?"

"Yes. I think it's time to go home. Won't you consider coming with us?"

"No...I can't. I've got too much invested in New Wellington and I think some good things are going to happen around here."

Oliver knew that Sam was in love with Rachel, but somehow he didn't seem too upset to know that she was working at the gaming hall. That wasn't like him. And Sam seemed to be pressing them both to leave.

Oliver touched his son's hand. "Son, I don't know what's going on, but be careful. Don't get hurt."

Sam smiled at his father. "I won't, Father. Believe me. You don't have anything to worry about. Things will work out just fine."

Oliver removed his hand and shook his head.

"You're still involved?" Oliver asked, leaving the words "with Rachel" unspoken.

Sam knew what he meant and shook his head. "I'm still involved."

"Will you write me with any news?" Oliver asked.

"Of course, Father. You'll be the first."

Rachel had been working at the hall for two weeks when she got her first break.

Walking from the office toward a booth overlooking the gaming room, she carried a list of inventory that didn't match up with what had been sold. She stopped short and cocked her ear toward the stall when she heard a conversation between Peter and Cabot Newgate.

"I tell you, Brogade, something's got to be done about Tanner," Newgate said, agitated.

"Such as?"

"I don't know, but he's run up a tab as long as your arm, not only of whiskey, but the girls."

"You know we give certain clients some liberties," Peter reminded him.

"One-thousand worth?"

"Is it that much now?"

"Yes."

"Hasn't he paid anything by currency?" Peter asked.

"No."

"Gold? Silver?"

"You know that specie is scarce in this area," Cabot jogged his memory.

"Any furs in trade?"

"He stays too drunk and too—er—occupied to concern himself about trapping or hunting."

"Surely he couldn't have drunk that much whiskey and slept with that many women."

"Get some sense about you, man," Cabot chided. "His gambling debts are the biggest part of it."

"Why wasn't I told this before?"

"I tried. But he was a friend of yours," Newgate sneered.

"Well, collect it, then," suggested Peter.

"I can't. Like I said, he doesn't have it."

"What do you propose we do about it?"

"I'd say it's time to do away with him."

"That's a little extreme, don't you think?"

"It's either that," Cabot said to Peter, "or take a chance that everyone will hear that we're an easy touch. That'll bring every slacker around."

Peter hesitated a moment, obviously not liking the alternative. "Well…do it discreetly," Peter finally directed. "Take Jeremiah with you. He can help bury the body. I don't suppose Holloway should be told about this?"

"Naw," replied Newgate. "That rich daddy of his wouldn't approve."

Horrified, Rachel thought for an instant that she was imagining things. She knew that Peter was callous, but to plan something like this was ruthless beyond what she'd known him to be.

She started to turn away when Peter stepped out of the stall and nearly collided with her. His eyebrows immediately drew together. "How long have you been here?" he asked.

Rachel steeled herself. She was sure guilt was written on her face, but if she could keep calm, she might survive the next few moments.

"What's that, Peter? I just wanted to show you a list of inventory. I have some questions about it."

Studying her for a few moments and then deciding that she hadn't overheard their conversation, he said, "Sure. Come back to the office. I've got some questions for you, too."

As they walked back, a fear began to throb in her throat. She was edgy beyond description. This was way beyond her expertise. Business dealings she could handle. But murder?

"Calm down," she told herself. "Don't let Peter suspect that you overheard that conversation or the murder just might turn out to be yours."

Walking into the office, Peter directed, "First of all, I want to see Tanner's account. I'm told he's run up quite a debt."

After Rachel jerkily shuffled through the accounts, she found, "Tanner, Clark." She handed it to Peter and he quickly scanned it.

"Hmm...five hundred...a hefty amount...but not one thousand. That sounds like Newgate—always exaggerating. If I hadn't needed his connections in Lexington...."

"What's that?" Rachel asked, projecting innocence on her face to the best of her ability.

"Nothing," Peter said, tossing the paper onto the desk. "Now...what's this about the inventory?"

She picked up her list again. "It doesn't match," Rachel said, pointing to her list of figures. "Here...see? This column is what should be in stock. This column...what actually is."

"That—!" Peter ejaculated, thinking about Cabot Newgate. "Can't trust anybody! I'll have to keep my eyes open to catch that thief! He's probably selling the stuff on his trips to Logan County! Whiskey is as valuable as gold in Kentucky!"

"Who are you talking about?" she asked.

Peter looked at Rachel as though he'd forgotten for a moment that she was there.

"Never mind—just keep me posted. I need a daily report."

Insistent that he drive her home in the dark, Sam was meeting Rachel every evening at Cherry Fork.

Relating the news she had heard that evening, Sam asked, "Who is this Tanner?"

"He's someone from Logan County who's been staying there for a bit. He's evidently some acquaintance of Peter and Cabot."

"And you say Newgate is planning to kill Tanner? All because of a gambling debt?"

"Yes. That's what they said. But I think there's more to it than that."

"What do you mean?"

"I overheard something the other night as I was leaving, but I didn't think much of it at the time."

"What was that?"

"It seems that Cabot and Tanner have been working together and selling whiskey in Logan County without Peter's knowledge. I heard them quarreling outside and Tanner accused Cabot of shorting his share of the profits. Tanner threatened to go to Peter about the matter. As I said, I didn't think much about it then."

"Hmm. I think it's time to bring someone else in."

"What do you mean? No one was supposed to know about Payne and now you and Pa know. And you want to let someone else know?" she asked incredulously.

"We need someone to check on this Tanner in Logan County. I think Gabe Roswell might be good for that. He's been a pretty rough character in the past. He'll fit in with that crowd and not draw much attention to himself."

"But, Sam," she cried, "Cabot Newgate is Abigail's father and he's the one who's planning the murder! Gabe is his son-in-law."

"I know. But I don't think Gabe will cut him any slack. He's pretty much against Newgate for upsetting Abigail so."

"Don't you think that will cause a rift in their marriage?"

Sam looked at her. "Are you more concerned about a rift than a man being murdered?"

"I suppose you're right," Rachel said, not entirely convinced.

"You wanted to see me, Sam?" Gabe Roswell asked as he stepped into Sam's office.

"Yes. Sit down, Gabe. I have a little problem and I think you may be able to solve it. You're aware what's going on at the gambling hall outside of town, aren't you?"

Gabe screwed up his face and spat out, "Definitely. That miserable crook! I could take Newgate apart for what he's done to Abigail."

"Well, there's a little matter of an intended murder that's about to occur and I need you to check up on someone in Logan County."

"What's the name?"

"Tanner."

"First name?"

"Clark."

"Does this have anything to do with Abigail?"

"Indirectly. It's her father that's supposed to do the killing."

Gabe's mouth turned down. "I knew that man was no good when we met on the trail. I never liked his bragging ways. Just put up with him for Abigail's sake."

"Yes, well...."

"Don't take any offense, Sam, and to be sure it's none of my business, but is Rachel involved in this?"

"In a way. She's the one who passed on the information. You see, she's working undercover. Brogade has threatened to harm her son if she doesn't cooperate with him. Mind you, all this has to be kept in strict confidence. Not even Abigail can know."

"I understand." Gabe slapped his knee. "I knew all that gossip was nothing but a lot of talk. Rachel's a good girl for all her peculiar ways."

"I've talked to the council and they've agreed to appoint you as sheriff. Are you willing to take the position? We'll need someone with the authority to do the arrest when the time comes."

"I understand. Sure, I'll take the job."

"When can you leave?"

"Whenever you want."

"How about today?"

"All right."

"Don't spend too much time there. No more than a couple of days. We may need you here. And it may be sooner than you think."

CHAPTER THIRTY-TWO

IT WAS APPROACHING FALL and the residents of New Wellington had planned a harvest festival, and folks from the surrounding area were invited to share in the festivities.

The long, trestle picnic tables were loaded with meat dishes, biscuits, vegetables from backyard gardens and pies made from fruit, along with cakes with the juice of ripened fruit dripping down their sides.

At dusk, the music began and partners came together to dance.

In the darkening twilight, Race Holloway stood in the shadows. He missed his home in Lexington. He missed decent folks, decent parties, and decent living. He was growing tired of the loud bawdiness of vulgar women, drunkenness, and men who would cut your throat for the slightest reason.

When Race caught sight of Claudia Stone, he was attracted to her right away. But as she darted from one dancing partner to another, he doubted that an opportunity would arise to meet her. He stood watching her for a long time and suddenly, as though she sensed someone was watching, she looked his way. He drew back further into the shadows, but she didn't look away. He gasped as he realized she was walking right toward him. He barely breathed.

Coming within three feet where he was hiding, she called apprehensively, "Is anyone there?"

Race pressed even closer against the side of the building.

"Hello," she called again. "Is anyone there?"

Silence.

A slight breeze carrying the promise of an early winter had arisen. She could smell him—smelled the mix of horses and the cologne he was wearing.

"I know there's someone there," she repeated, drawing her wrap closer about her. Claudia was on the verge of going for help when Race let out his breath and stepped slowly out of the shadows.

"You're mighty bold to come over here in the dark like this, miss. You should be more careful."

Ignoring his advice, "Who are you?" she asked.

Nervously removing his hat, he answered, "I'm—I'm Race Holloway, miss."

"Race Holloway? I don't believe I've met you before. Do you live around here or perhaps Mission Point?"

He was ashamed to tell her. Ashamed to tell a fine girl like her that he lived at Brogade's Palace. "No—yes—well—sort of," Race stammered. He was glad it was dark so she couldn't see his face.

"Sort of?" she responded brusquely. "What does that mean?"

"Well, miss, I'm staying at Brogade's outside of town," cringing as he said it.

She could barely make out his features. But the light from the lanterns was enough that she could tell he was good-looking.

"Well, Mr. Holloway. Why don't you move closer to the party?"

"Oh, no, miss. I couldn't do that," he said as he fingered his hat. "They—well," he gave a short laugh, "it's just better that I stay here, miss."

She looked back at the crowd. If her father and grandfather knew she was out here with a man from the bawdy house, well…part of her shuddered as to what they would do, yet—part of her was adventurous.

Claudia turned back and saw in the faint light on his face that he was watching her with interest. She was bored. Eligible young men her age were scarce, even among the new arrivals in town. Other than Sam, her choices had been immature boys or much older men and she longed for beaux. And if fulfilling that longing meant chatting with men from the bawdy house, then she supposed it couldn't hurt—just this once anyway.

"Well," she began, making up her mind to stay, "since you won't come to the party, Mr. Holloway, let's sit here in front of the store and talk awhile."

What luck! Never in his wildest dreams had he ever imagined that a beautiful girl like her, and a nice one at that, would offer such a thing. In Lexington maybe…but not here in New Wellington.

Moving quickly to assist her to the bench, he was careful to sit as close to his own edge of the seat as he could without actually falling off.

Finally settled, she asked, "Why do they call you Race? Is that your real name?"

"No," he answered. "They call me Race because I love to race horses."

"Hmm. You're not from around here then, Mr. Holloway?"

"No. I was born and raised in Charleston, and my parents moved to Lexington a few years ago. To please me, I assume, as I have such a fondness for horses. And Lexington is known for its excellent breeding stock, you know."

"Yes, I know." Claudia answered.

"The Buford family owns the winning horses there," he informed her. "What I wouldn't give to have a horse like one of their stock!" He looked off into the distance as though the answer lay in the darkened landscape beyond. Lexington, he was thinking about.

It was clear where Race's heart was and it wasn't working at the bawdy house.

Claudia hesitated, then: "Are you a partner in that—er—gambling establishment outside of town?"

"Not me," he admitted as he glanced at the hat in his hand. "It's my father. I'm only here to look after his interests. He's only a small partner, really. He owns ten percent. Brogade owns seventy and Newgate, twenty."

"You know the town doesn't approve of such a place."

Race shrugged his shoulders. "You know the old saying…to each his own."

Hearing a small gasp from Claudia and looking up to see the look of astonishment on her face, he hurriedly apologized, "I'm sorry, miss. I didn't mean it quite like that."

"So you approve of the goings-on at the hall?" she asked a little testily.

"Not really. I didn't want Brogade and Cabot Newgate to know yet, but I've been thinking about leaving for Lexington soon. Newgate assured Father that this was to be a hotel promoting the mineral springs. Father will be outraged, for sure, when I tell him that it's nothing but a—"

Race flushed a little. "Sorry again, miss. I've just been putting it off."

"So—when are you leaving for Lexington, Mr. Holloway?"

Race fixed her with a keen eye. "Would it matter to you?" he asked pointedly.

Claudia smiled ever so slightly.

"Could be," she answered coyly.

"Well, then, probably in a week or so. Newgate's been talking about making a trip to Lexington to raise some more funds. So I'll go with him then."

"I'm glad to hear that type of lifestyle doesn't meet your standards."

"May I ask you a question, miss?"

Claudia nodded yes.

"What's your name?"

"Claudia. Claudia Stone."

Raising his brows, he asked, "As in the Stone family of Stone Valley?"

"The very ones," she answered a little smugly. "My father is Claude Stone and my grandfather is the doctor."

"Hmm...I'd heard some news around town about you."

"News? About me?" Claudia asked, surprised. She leaned to the side so she could get a full view of his face.

Race cringed. A gentleman didn't act so forward like that to a lady, especially a lady like her.

At his silence, she asked again in a voice that had turned decidedly frigid. "You said you had heard some news...about me?"

He took a deep breath to steady himself and filled his lungs with cool night air.

"Yes." Race twirled his hat anxiously in his hands and debated whether to get up and leave. But he was drawn to her and in the end decided to stay.

"Well, since you've told me that much," Claudia said, her curiosity aroused, as she poised on the edge of the seat, "would you mind telling me what this news is?"

No sense holding back now. "I've heard that you and Sam Spencer have a special relationship."

Claudia laughed, visibly relaxing. "Well, I want to inform you, Mr. Holloway, that Mr. Spencer and I do not entertain any relationship...special or otherwise. We're merely friends."

Race breathed a sigh of relief. "Good."

"To be frank," Claudia continued, "Sam already has an interest in someone. It's Rachel Templeton."

He grew wide-eyed. "Rachel Templeton? The girl who works in Brogade's office? Brogade's ex-wife?"

"Yes," she admitted, a little peeved, "that's the one. Some call her 'The Attorney's Lady'."

With an airy wave of her hand, she said, "Oh...Sam tries to make people think he is only the executor of her estate."

Lifting her chin a little, she continued, "But I know better. Sam's head-over-heels in love with her and I've heard that they're meeting secretly every night at Cherry Fork."

"Huh?" Race asked, surprised. The wheels were clicking in Race's mind. He was sure that Peter didn't know that little piece of news. This could turn nasty, he thought. Peter acted like Rachel was his girl...his wife, in fact. At least, that's what he always referred to her as.

If anyone made a comment about her that was out of bounds at the hall, Peter was ready to take them apart. True, he'd noticed that Rachel acted scared of Peter at times. To Race, it seemed that she was playing a dangerous game.

Claudia interrupted his thoughts. "I've also been told that her father, John Winslow, has left for Lexington, himself."

"Winslow, did you say?"

"Yes. Will you be staying in Lexington or returning?"

His heart catapulted at her question. "I'll return if Father decides to send me back...just as soon as I can."

CHAPTER THIRTY-THREE

JOHN WINSLOW WAS ABOUT TWO MILES from Lexington when his horse pulled up lame. Stepping down from the saddle, he moved to inspect the leg his horse was favoring. Broken! It must have been that hole he stepped in.

They had been together a long time...through all his trips to Kentucky and Virginia. He didn't have a name except 'Horse', but they were a perfect fit. With just a little pressure from John's knee, Horse anticipated John's every move.

He hated to put the animal down, but it had to be done. Unsaddling the horse, he walked up to the animal and rubbed its ears one last time.

"Sorry, Horse," John softly said, "you've been a good companion. But I've got to do it."

John moved to the front and lifting his pistol, with one merciful shot, put the animal out of his misery.

The horse was dead. He looked down at him and found tears in his eyes, although he wasn't a crying man.

Walking up McKanon Road, John entered Lexington. Crossing the gangway over Main Street, he marveled that most of the buildings and homes of this well-known city were still made of logs.

New Wellington, in its infancy, he reflected with pride, boasted many frame buildings. Chiefly because of the efforts of Will Templeton, he reminded himself.

Stopping a pedestrian, he asked where he might find accommodations.

"Postlethwait's," he answered, "or try Megowan's here on Main."

His saddle was weighing heavy on his shoulder, so he decided on Megowan's.

It only took a few days for John to find out what he needed to know. Cabot Newgate was partners with Nathan Holloway—but not the kind of partnership that Holloway thought.

John had just divulged the details to Holloway.

"My son Race has been involved with such goings-on?" Nathan Holloway asked John.

"Not really," John answered. "Oh, he was intrigued with the whole thing for a while, but I don't think his heart was really in it."

Nathan snorted in disgust. "I'm sending a post and bringing him home right away."

"Pardon me, but I think the most important thing right now is getting the whole mess cleared up. The prostitutes are disturbing the ladies of the town. A bold lot they are, parading down Main Street in broad daylight. And then, there's the matter of Clark Tanner."

"Yes. You're right," Nathan thoughtfully admitted. "What do you want me to do?"

"Whatever your son knows, he needs to come forward with it."

"Yes, yes, of course."

Cabot Newgate and Race Holloway arrived in Lexington just after John and Nathan had met.

John decided to disappear into the background and return to New Wellington.

As Cabot Newgate knew John Winslow from the Wilderness Road before he was taken back to South Carolina to stand trial for theft, it wouldn't do for Newgate to find him investigating the activities at Brogade Palace.

John purchased a horse from Cahall's farm and was preparing to return to New Wellington. He had saddled his horse in the stable when something shifted on the straw-covered floor. His ears alert, he froze and inched his hand down to his pistol. Turning his head, he squinted into the shadows of a nearby stall.

"Someone there?" he cautiously asked, barely breathing.

John moved one step away from the horse and heard the shifting sound again.

"Who's there?" he demanded as he pulled out his pistol.

More shifting and then a figure straightened up and slowly stepped out.

"No need for that, Winslow" Newgate said. "I'm just here to talk."

John doubted that. Sizing Newgate up and cautiously lowering his pistol, John stated, "So talk."

"You've been to Holloway," stated Newgate coldly.

John said nothing, but kept his hand ready to aim and fire. He didn't trust Newgate. He was like a rattlesnake and his tone, reminiscent of hissing, made it clear that he was about to strike.

"Been over there messing up things for me," accused Newgate.

"How'd you get out of jail?"

"I have friends," Newgate offered.

"It appears that you do," admitted John.

Newgate bared his teeth. "I had a pretty good thing going and you had to muddle up everything for me."

"What made you think you could double-cross Brogade?" John touted.

Newgate's eyes narrowed. "What do you mean?" he asked.

"It's all over, Newgate. Brogade knows you're cheating him, selling his liquor out from under him."

"How—?"

"Never mind how I know," John said in a quiet, but confident voice. "And what made you think that Holloway's own son would go along with your underhanded dealings?" John asked.

"Well...it was either go along or—" Newgate accidently let slip out.

"Or what?" John snapped. "Kill him like you planned for Clark Tanner?"

For a moment it looked like fear in Newgate's eyes. But it wasn't there long. In its place appeared hate.

"How did you know?" Newgate demanded.

"I have my sources," John replied as Rachel's face flashed before him.

Newgate's brow drew together in thought. How could Winslow have known? Then his eyes flashed and he uttered, "Rachel!"

John offered no denial and Newgate swore under his breath, "That little—"

"You're through, Newgate," John interrupted, "You, Brogade, and your whole scheme—the prostitutes, black marketing the liquor, the whole bit."

John's warning was cut short as the door to the stable swung open. Instead of another patron, Megowan himself entered the stable.

"What the—?" Megowan uttered, seeing the pistol in John's hand and sensing the standoff between the two men.

John's head swung around to see who had stepped in and Newgate, taking advantage of the distraction, lifted his own pistol and quickly squeezed the trigger, hitting John in the chest.

At the report of the gun and the smell of smoke, John dropped his pistol and clutching his chest, stumbled back against the wall of the stall.

Quickly swinging his large frame into the saddle, Newgate yelled, "Hyah," as he snapped the reins, hunkered down low in the saddle, and kneed the horse. Racing through the stable door, Newgate released his foot from the stirrup long enough to shove it into Megowan's shoulder, knocking him against the door.

In the dust of the departing horse, Megowan gathered his wits about him, pushed away from the door, and rushed to where John was lying on the floor, writhing from a wound that was pouring blood.

"Dear, Lord!" Megowan said as he locked eyes with John. "You're hurt bad, man."

As much as John wanted to speak, no sound came from his lips, and he found himself contorting his shoulders and clutching his chest in a frenzied effort to relieve the pain.

"Stay still," Megowan ordered. "I'm going for the doctor."

After Megowan left, even in the state John was in, he saw his pistol was lying in easy reach. What about Rachel? And Payne? Closing his bloodied hand on the barrel and pulling it toward him, he struggled to get up He needed to get to New Wellington.

But then, as darkness began to overtake him, he fell forward, still clutching the gun.

CHAPTER THIRTY-FOUR

BROGADE'S PALACE WAS IN FULL SWING when Newgate arrived back in New Wellington. He needed a bath, but that could wait. He had more important business to take care of.

Tethering his horse to the rail in back, he pulled one of his pistols and quietly climbed the steps to Peter's office. Pausing outside the door, he slowly turned the knob. Peeking through the crack in the door, he saw Rachel sitting at the desk and Peter bent over her. Engrossed in paperwork, they never heard him slip into the room.

"I'm back, Brogade," Newgate announced.

Swinging around, Peter caught sight of the pistol aimed at him.

"What's all this?" Peter asked as his eyes focused intensely on the barrel of the gun.

"Thought you could put one over on me, didn't you, Brogade?" Newgate accused.

Peter blinked, but kept his eyes riveted on the firearm. Pulling his eyes to look into Newgate's narrowed ones, he asked, "What are you talking about, Cabot? Put what over on you?"

"You and your little honey, there." Newgate spat out as he nodded Rachel's way.

Newgate was in a dangerous frame of mind, Peter saw. It would take some doing to calm him down.

Peter tried bored impatience. "Explain yourself, Cabot."

"You know exactly what I mean, Brogade. Thought you could pin Tanner's murder on me alone, didn't you? Didn't you know that your little ex-wife there was acting like a spy on our whole operation?"

Peter's blood instantly boiled. "Be careful what you say about Rachel, Newgate."

"Be careful what you say about Rachel," Newgate mimicked. "You were always blind when it came to her. Look at her," Newgate demanded. "It's written all over her face. She's guilty as sin."

Peter turned to look at Rachel and couldn't overlook the fact that she looked scared. But then, who wouldn't when someone had a pistol pulled on you?

Newgate spoke to Rachel. "Tell him. Tell him just what you've been doing. Spying and reporting what you've seen and heard."

Addressing Peter again, he asked, "Did you know that Winslow spilled everything about the whole operation to Nathan Holloway? And that he's making plans to shut us down?"

Rachel hadn't known that her father was in Lexington. What was he doing there? What was going on that could threaten Payne? Everything had spiraled out of control, and she began to feel sick to her stomach.

"Well...let me tell you, missy, you can't tell your father anything anymore," Newgate continued, his face hard. "John Winslow is dead," he said triumphantly.

Rachel's face went white as a sheet.

"Pa's...dead?"

"Yes," his face contorted into an ugly smile and he said, "just like you will be."

She jumped to her feet, breathing hard. It couldn't be true. Not Pa. Her jaw trembled and she clenched her teeth to steady it.

"That's right, missy," Newgate snarled. "Dead. I shot him right through the heart. John Winslow, the great scout! He won't be doing any more talking."

He took two steps toward her. "And I'm going to do the same to you."

Rachel shrank back, frightened by the savage glitter in his eyes.

"Say your prayers," Newgate growled, pacing another step closer. "You're about to die."

Say her prayers? Scenes of others in their final moments feverishly uttering final words flashed before her. Ransom's words of endearment to her, his instructions to Sam, and her mother's last, feeble caress and utterance: "God won't put more upon you than you can bear."

But no entreaty of her own came to her mind. As though frozen in time, she watched as Newgate raised the weapon, aiming for her forehead.

At the last second, Peter lunged in front of Rachel as Newgate's pistol fired. Thrown back against her, sending her reeling into the wall, Peter grasped frantically at the desk, then slid down its side to the floor.

Newgate was stunned momentarily. Aiming for Rachel, he'd shot the wrong person. After regaining his sensibilities, Newgate unholstered his other pistol.

Coldly assessing her, he shifted to his side and widened his stance. He was turning his head towards her and raising the pistol slowly and deliberately, when a shot rang out from behind him.

Newgate's eyes opened wide, his arm slid down to his side, and the pistol fell from his hand, making a muffled sound on the carpet where it dropped. A second later, he fell as well. He was dead.

Her hand over her mouth, Rachel looked in astonishment beyond where Newgate had stood, and there stood her quiet protector. Jeremiah slowly lowered the gun he had just fired.

No one had seen him come in.

The whole scene was a nightmare. It couldn't be real—or if it was real, then the whole world had gone crazy. How could she, just a few minutes ago, have believed that everything was under control? No imminent threat. No danger.

Now she was in a dream—a dream too terrible to be real. Delayed reaction set in and her knees began to buckle.

Then she heard a moan.

The sound drawing her out of her daze, Rachel looked down to see where the groan had come from.

Peter's upper body was hidden by the desk, but his legs moved.

In slow motion, Rachel came from behind the desk, stepped over Peter's long, twitching legs. and crouched where he lay dying.

"Rachel," Peter clutched at her hand, "I've been shot. I'm not going to live."

Rachel hesitated, debating whether a kind lie would be better than the truth. She searched her mind for something to say, but no words came to her. She didn't answer.

The room was warm, but she was cold inside.

"I'm not going to make it," he told her. "Oh, dear God, have mercy on me," Peter pleaded to the heavens.

As though a semblance of sanity returned to him in his last tortured moments, he felt the need to set accounts right with her

"Rachel, you have to know—this place is willed to you. Do with it what you want. Burn it to the ground, for all I care. I've been crazy with jealousy," Peter confessed, struggling to stay alert. "I knew you didn't love me when I married you. You see, I knew about Ransom. I wanted to take you away from Wellington and all the memories you shared with him. I thought if you left with me, left the Templeton family and Ransom, you would forget about him and learn to love me. But you wouldn't," he said painfully as he momentarily closed his eyes, "wouldn't leave."

The bitterness in his voice spoke of a raw, unhealed wound that had been festering for a long time. Peter's face twisted with pain and he fought to hold life in his body a few more moments as Rachel hardly breathed, waiting for his next words.

"After you left me," he muttered, watching her again, "I was angry. I wandered from place to place, trying to forget you. But I couldn't and I had to find you again. When I blackmailed you into working with me, I thought I could make you care. I tried, but you just didn't."

He coughed a dying, rasping cough.

Peter swallowed hard.

"Rachel, I would never have harmed Payne," Peter hoarsely reasoned. "I only wanted you—wanted you with me. You probably don't believe me, but I love you. I just didn't know how to show it." Raising his eyes to the ceiling, "I have so much to be forgiven for," Peter prayed. "Dear God, please forgive me."

Death was approaching. Realization of it forced his eyes open wide. "Rachel...."

And with that said, Peter was gone an instant before his eyes closed.

Looking at the hands that had abused her in the past, it was over—finally over. Peter was forever out of her life.

But it wasn't real, surely not. Peter, who still had the color of life on his face, wasn't dead. Not really. He would get up. She knew he would. She stared at his still face. Then she removed her hand from his motionless one and laid it on his chest. There was no movement, no heartbeat, no heaving of his torso.

Rachel could not accuse him now, could not rant and rave at him anymore. Perhaps, in his own twisted way, he had some feelings for her. He certainly proved it by taking that fatal shot intended for her.

Like a candle that lighted the room, she understood him now. Saw clearly that jealousy had driven him to do the things he had done to her—jealousy driven to excess because it could not really possess. Did it justify what he had done? No. Did she believe he loved her? No. Love didn't do the things that he did to her.

A chapter in her life was now closed. Odd, that Rachel should feel such sadness. A little girl had been born from their relationship. Lived and died. Peter could have had a wonderful life, she thought. But bent on living life by his cruel way…it had come to this.

You reap what you sow. Yes, the reaping time had come.

Rachel hoped fervently that God had heard his prayer.

She had never hated Peter. But she had never loved him, either.

Sliding her hand down the front of his shirt, she lifted it, turned the palm up, and studied her bloodstained hand. It should have repelled her, but it didn't. There was dullness in her mind now. A dullness that she knew from past experience would give way to the pain looming as a long-time acquaintance, waiting to gain entrance into her thoughts and feelings.

Death! As she sat motionless, Rachel was enveloped by a sense of doom. Every death she encountered drove something indescribable and unexplainable deeper inside of her. Rachel only knew that she desperately wanted to run away. Run away from sorrow.

For a few seconds her thoughts twirled and she entertained the notion that she would escape to somewhere, anywhere. But she couldn't run. There was Payne. Pa was gone and Payne was her only family now. She had to stay for him. Bowing her head and closing her eyes for a few seconds, she tried to squeeze back the tears, but in spite of her efforts, they were soon trickling down her cheeks.

A rebel was what Sam had called her. She didn't feel much like that now.

Rachel finally raised her head and looked at Jeremiah. He, in his own quiet way, had always looked after her at that place of ill repute, often appearing out of nowhere in difficult days at the Palace. She had come to rely on his presence. Always standing in the shadows, he had waited. Waited for the day he knew would come.

His eyes reflected the kindness she had always shown him.

Rachel smiled a wavering smile. Jeremiah's own smile reflected hers. There was no need for words. She would be all right...now.

CHAPTER THIRTY-FIVE

JEREMIAH LED SAM AND GABE to where Clark Tanner's body was buried in the forest. There, Peter Brogade and Cabot Newgate were buried, also.

Standing at the mound of fresh earth heaped up over Peter's grave, Rachel couldn't cry. She never wanted his life to end like this. Not such a violent death and not so young. She knew so little about him. Had never known who his family was or where they were. Were a father and mother somewhere wondering where their son was? He had been her husband such a brief time. Had it been just two years ago when they exchanged vows?

"Pa is gone" was the phrase that sounded continually in her mind. It was a struggle to get up in the morning. He had been the light of her life as she grew up, basking in his praise and approval. The memories crowded her mind from morning to night until she thought she would go mad. Her only consolation was Payne. She had been willing to risk it all for him. And now he was safe.

Once Frank and Louise learned Rachel's reason for working at Brogade's Palace, they agreed to stay at North Star for another year.

Louise brooded about Rachel. It wasn't like her to be morose. She had always rebounded quickly from any setback. But not now.

It had been two weeks since the shootings at the Palace. Sam came calling every day at North Star, but Rachel refused to see him. Finally, at Louise's insistence, Rachel agreed to an outing with him, just to pacify her.

When she descended the stairs, Sam's heart caught in his throat. Simply dressed, hair released from the popular coif she had been wearing and now flowing down her back, she looked the same as the first time they met. Rachel looked younger than the eighteen she now was.

In her eyes, however, was age beyond her years. The light was gone. With everything within him, he vowed to put the love of life back into those dark eyes again.

Stopping at a ridge, they disembarked from the buggy and stood overlooking the valley. The river cutting through it was flowing swiftly as though by its momentum it could hold back the freeze of the coming winter. Rachel folded her arms as though scooping the spectrum before her into them. She took a deep breath and slowly released it. The autumn scene before her filled Rachel with peace and, as always, when in the outdoors, she felt a little strength returning as her spirits lifted somewhat. Feeling comforted by the view before her, a hint of a smile tugged at the corners of her mouth and she was glad Sam had brought her here. This was her favorite spot in the whole valley.

Not speaking for a long while, Sam watched every move she made, every feeling that fluttered over her youthful face. The last few months he had waited for the right moment. The moment when he was sure she would say yes to him. Several times, in emotion-filled flashes, he had nearly blurted it out to her. He knew she loved him…knew it as sure as she was standing with him on the ridge. Now was that time.

"Rachel," he began and then hesitated. "I know you've gone through a lot lately and probably feel worn out emotionally."

That was true. She did.

"However, I have something I want to ask you."

Her arms still folded, she turned a quizzical brow to him.

"I'm asking you to marry me."

As blunt as that. No passionate words of love. No ardent overtures.

After a few seconds, when his words finally registered, she blinked…hard.

"Marry?" she numbly asked.

"Yes. We could have a good marriage."

She nearly laughed out loud. This man, whom she had so much trouble with, wanted to marry her?

"That's a good joke, Sam." Turning her attention back to the view, she said indifferently, "But really, I'm not in the mood just now."

"It's not a joke," Sam said quietly.

Rachel looked at him…looked hard. Sam wasn't joking. He was serious…dead serious. There was a bland look on his unsmiling face, but still, he was serious.

Suddenly, her heart beat a little faster. Admitting to herself, not long ago, that she loved him, she had made up her mind that she would never enter another marriage. At least, not one where there was love only on one side. Sam never said he loved her—never hinted in any way, except by look.

Rachel answered thoughtfully, "I've had enough people leave my life."

She unfolded her arms and exhaled a deep sigh. "To tell you the truth, Sam, I'm not up to it anymore."

"To—?" Sam asked.

"To losing the people in my life," she explained.

Rachel brushed a strand of hair from her forehead.

"Besides...I'll never marry again," she informed him.

"Yes, you will," he stated emphatically. "And you'll marry me."

Rachel chafed at that. Marry him indeed! He was always telling her what to do.

"I should have married Hayden," she remarked offhandedly, a part of her wanting to stir up the old strife.

"But you didn't love him," he remarked.

"Love doesn't matter," she said, but then instantly thought about Peter. It mattered to him. The lack of it drove him to do things out of rage.

"Doesn't matter?" Sam asked.

Rachel looked down and merely shrugged her shoulders. The conversation was getting too personal, and she debated whether to start for the buggy.

For the last year, since Sam had known her, his love for her burned hot within him. First... while she was Ransom's wife...then, his widow...then, as executor and guardian of her estate. He endured her tirades, all the time loving her—wanting her.

He couldn't hold back any longer.

Sam reached for Rachel and pulled her into his arms. He lifted her chin, his eyes blazing as they commanded her own startled eyes to face the fire in his heart shining like shafts of light through his eyes. He covered her lips with a fierce and passionate kiss, then forced himself to restrain his emotions and feathered her jaw line with soft kisses.

"Tell me again it doesn't matter," he murmured passionately.

All of the pent-up emotion of the last few months within Rachel burst like a dam and she began to cry. She tried to pull away.

But he wouldn't let her. Placing hands on both sides of her face, Sam forced her to look at him.

"Tell me you don't love me. Tell me!" he demanded.

She was sobbing. "What do you want from me...a confession?"

"Yes! I want a confession! For once in your life—for the *first* time in your life—face the truth. You love me! Tell me!"

Wordlessly, Rachel tried to wrench his hands from her face. He refused to release her.

"Tell me!" he said again.

"Yes!" she nearly shouted.

And with that answer, came peace and she ceased to struggle. She did love him. She truly did. But on the heels of that answer, came the echo of his promise to Ransom.

"But I won't have your pity," she stated simply.

Sam drew back, dropped his hands, and blinked hard. "Pity?" he incredulously asked. "You think I asked you out of pity?"

She didn't answer.

"You little fool," he continued. "I have loved you and love you now. I just couldn't tell you. You've been so angry at me."

She hiccupped slightly as she brushed the tears from her face. "Well...after all, you did make that promise to Ransom."

"Yes, I did," he admitted. "And I've kept it. But did it ever occur to you that I went beyond that promise?"

Rachel looked at him, confused.

"Why do you think I was so jealous of Hayden?"

"You were jealous?" she asked, wide-eyed. "I thought you were just giving me a hard time."

Sam laughed. "You ninny—you can't tell when love is staring you right in the face. I'm telling you here and now, I love you. I love you with all my heart. Always have."

"Always?"

Looking her straight in the eyes, he answered somberly, "Always."

Did he love her when she was married to Ransom? Suddenly, she knew. He did. Now she understood. Understood why he had kept his distance from her on the journey here. It was as though she was seeing Sam for the first time. She understood everything now. Those few times she had seen the longing in his eyes. He loved her— protected her—kept her life on the right track.

"Did Pa know you love me?" she whispered.

"Yes. He did. And if it's any consolation at all…he approved."

Sam loved her. He said so. She didn't know whether to laugh or cry again. But could they get along? He didn't let her get away with anything. She'd been able to get her way with Ransom—but Sam?

"But you expect too much of me!" Rachel protested.

He smiled. "You don't have to be afraid of what I expect you to be. I'm pulling the best out of you. I refuse to settle for half-measures. You've needed someone to stand with you. I'm the one God has sent into your life. Don't you understand that?"

"But I'm different than other women you have known."

"Exactly."

"I'm not versed in social graces—nor do I want to be. I want to be what I am—not what others expect me to be. I don't want anyone to force me to change."

"I'm not trying to change you. I'm trying to set you free to be who you are—the person God made you to be." Sam took her hand and said gently, "God has put goodness in you, Rachel that others need. They need someone who is real—not a phony. Together, God will use us to bring to pass his plans and purpose."

Dare she hope for some happiness? Rachel finally agreed and said yes.

Dining at North Star, Sam and Rachel made plans for their upcoming nuptials.

"Do I have enough funds for such a big wedding?" Rachel asked.

"Forget it. I'm paying for it," Sam answered. "Your first two weddings were small affairs overshadowed by the disapproval of others."

Touching her hand, he smiled and said, "I want our marriage started right, with the consent and attendance of all our friends."

There was a knock on the door. Louise answered it and appeared at the dining room door with a look of disapproval on her face. "Rachel, there's a Mr. Race Holloway here, asking to see you."

"Race Holloway?" Rachel asked, glancing at Sam. "What's *he* doing here?"

Sam grimaced and shrugged his shoulders.

"Well, then, Louise. Show him in."

Rachel rose from her seat as Race entered the room. Sam rose also and went to lean against the fireplace, cautious at Race's appearance.

Race crossed the floor and gave a slight bow. Rachel nodded and said, "Mr. Holloway. What can I do for you?"

A grin creased the corners of Race's mouth and he said, "It's more like what I can do for you. I heard the news in town that Cabot Newgate said your father is dead."

She nodded again.

He reached into his coat pocket. "I have a message for you from your father, John Winslow." Extracting the paper, he handed it to her.

"When he was alive?" she asked.

"No. No. Go ahead and read it."

Confused, Rachel took the letter from his hand and unfolded it. Leaning down to the candles burning on the table, she placed the letter next to the light. Reading it, she gasped and placed a hand on her chest.

Looking up at Race, she incredulously asked, "Pa is alive?"

"Yes, ma'am, he is."

She sat down, the candlelight falling on her white, bewildered face.

"But Cabot Newgate said he killed Pa."

"That's not true, Mrs. Templeton. Oh, Newgate thought he killed him. Mr. Winslow suffered a serious gunshot wound to his chest and was unconscious for several days. He's still recuperating in Lexington at my father's home, but the doctor says he's going to be just fine. Mr. Winslow's been mighty worried about you and Payne. That's why he sent me with that letter."

Rachel's heart sang. Pa was alive! She turned to Sam, happy tears threatening to spill down her cheeks and beamed the biggest smile she had smiled in a long time.

"Thank you, Race," Sam said gratefully.

Race nodded.

"Ma'am," he said, addressing Rachel again, "I'll be leaving for Lexington day after tomorrow and if you like, I could deliver any message you might have."

Sam pushed away from the fireplace and answered, "Thanks, Race. Come by my office tomorrow and Mrs. Templeton will have her letter ready."

With Race gone, Sam took Rachel in his arms and asked, "Happy?"

"Oh, yes!" she answered enthusiastically, "Pa is alive, Payne is safe, and we are to be married!"

He smiled at her and said, "My rebel lady. The lady of North Star."

About the Author

A graduate of Chatfield College and from a family of several ministers, Donna Whitaker has pastored several churches, and served as evangelist, missionary, songwriter, recording artist, musician, and teacher. Speaking at various venues, she has also served as spokeswoman and praise and worship leader with Aglow International, the women's division of The Full Gospel Businessmen's Association.

Donna's own family has a history in the area her novels are set in. Of Scottish descent and the well-known Sinclair family, Donna can trace her ancestor sailing on the ship Loyalty to North America in 1699 and follow her family's progress from Virginia to Adair County, Kentucky in the very early 1800's. Church and courthouse records document Alexander Sinclair, her 4th great grandfather, as an ordained minister of that county.

On her maternal side, Donna is descended from Brigadier General Jesse Richardson, a Revolutionary War soldier who also served under General George Rogers Clark. One of the first settlers of Pulaski County, Kentucky, General Richardson was elected to the Kentucky State Legislature as the first senator of Pulaski and Cumberland Counties in 1800.

Interacting with people from many walks of life has given Donna an understanding of people and helped to make her an effective storyteller.

Donna resides in southern Ohio.

Donna may be contacted at donnajeanwhitaker@gmail.com